Crown Queens

Book 3 of The Soiled Dove Sagas

Lori Beasley Bradley

This is a work of fiction. While some historic figures as well as locations are mentioned, they have been fictionalized and the sole responsibility of the author. No part of this novel may be reproduced unless with written permission from the author except short excerpts for promotional use.

ISBN: 13: 978-1532854828

Chapter 1

November 2, 1878

"You're one of them whores from Dodge City," the man said confidently with an arched gray brow. "You work in the cribs down by the tracks, don't you?" Hiram Garrison asked Roxie North rudely again for the hundredth time since he'd joined the coach at Fort Dodge. Roxie suspected he'd been asked to leave the Fort for cheating at cards as she knew he'd been asked to leave most of the gambling establishments in Dodge City. His traveling clothes were shabby, but clean and though Roxie would have preferred to ride in silence, she supposed it could have been worse. Yesterday they'd shared the coach with a young couple and their colicky infant that when not screaming was filling its diapers and the coach with a foul stench.

"I used to be," Roxie replied curtly, "but not anymore."

Roxie sat in the swaying coach, staring aimlessly out the window at the passing drab, dusty scenery. She'd never been this far south on the Cimarron trail. She'd never been south of Dodge City at all in her few years there, but a letter had come from her dearest friend, Mattie Wallace Kirby and she hadn't wasted any time making arrangements for a coach and the six-week trip from Kansas and across the Arizona Territory to Prescott, the Territorial capital where Mattie lived.

Roxie glanced up from Mattie's letter to eye her traveling companion as he lit another cigar and teased her with the smoke. She'd ignored Hiram Garrison's last offer of one of the tightly rolled little cigars because Roxie suspected he expected more than she had been willing to give in return for a few smokes.

"Come on now, girl," Garrison said as he inhaled deeply, "tell me true. Are you really riding this stage all to way to Arizona?"

"That's right," she said and refolded Mattie's letter to tuck back into its envelope. "My friend lost her baby to an illness and needs me." The coach's wheels hit a rut and jolted Roxie as she attempted to slip the envelope into her velvet reticule.

The day had started out cool, but as the afternoon progressed the coach had become stuffy and Garrison's continued smoking left Roxie breathless and wondering if she dared open the sash to let some fresh air into the rocking rig. Unfortunately, thick red dust would accompany any fresh air, voiding any positive effects. She finally gave up on getting the letter back into her bag and settled for waving it in front of her face as a fan instead.

"Hell of a ride to hold the hand of a grieving friend," Garrison said incredulously with a raised white eyebrow and a shake of his sweaty head. "Don't she have a husband for that?"

"Son-of-a-bitch up and left her," Roxie huffed as she fanned the blue smoke from Garrison's cigar out of her face. The breeze felt good as it cooled the perspiration trickling down her neck.

"Not very gentlemanly of him," Garrison said and offered her another smoke.

"Gentleman is not a word I'd ever use to describe Joshua Kirby." Roxie took the cigar he'd taken from his pocket to hold out to her and put it between her dry lips. He offered his cigar and she took it too light hers. She inhaled deeply until the tip glowed red. She handed the half-consumed cigar back to Garrison, who rested it between his nicotine-stained fingers.

"Are you about done with your readin' now, Miss Roxie?" Garrison asked as he moved to take a seat beside her in the bouncing coach. He boldly slipped a hand onto Roxie's knee and gave it a familiar squeeze. "You never did answer me as to whether or not you might consider movin' down to Cimarron to ply your trade to the cowpokes and gaming men down there."

Roxie raised an eyebrow at the too-familiar man and shifted her knee so his hand fell away. "I've told you a dozen times, Mr. Garrison, that I'm on my way to Arizona to visit a friend. I don't *ply* the Trade any longer."

"That's a mighty long way to travel," he repeated and scooted closer until the shoulders of his worn suit coat rubbed against the shoulder of her crisp poplin traveling suit. "I spent some time down in Yuma," he sighed and rolled his watery eyes. "I can't say as I'd recommend it." The man reached into his pocket and produced two more little brown cigars. He put one into his mouth and offered the other to Roxie. "It's hotter than Lucifer's kitchen down there and rains next to never. The damned Apaches are everywhere and," he said as he struck a Lucifer on the door frame and lit his cigar, "you can't find a good bottle of bourbon anywhere." He narrowed his eyes and pinched his brow. "Damned Mescal is all they serve."

Roxie rolled her eyes and tucked the unlit cigar into her jacket pocket. She reached into her drawstring bag for her silver flask. She took a draw on her smoke and handed Garrison the flask. His eyes brightened as he uncorked it and tipped it up. After a long swallow he handed the depleted flask back to Roxie. She took a sip of the Tennessee whiskey and returned it to her bag. She would have to refill it in Cimarron and hoped the St. James was the gambler's ultimate destination. He'd been regaling Roxie with his tales of card games played in every major city west of the Mississippi and The St. James Hotel in Cimarron was noted for its gaming room.

"You're a fine-lookin' woman, Miss Roxie," he said as he exhaled blue smoke into the coach. "You could do well in Cimarron. The St. James is a very lovely hotel." His hand crept up her leg and he bent to breathe into her ear. "You could do *very* well there. I'm certain of it." His tongue began to trace the curve of her dainty ear. "There aren't many white whores down there. The cowpokes don't mind the Mex cunny, but those of us with more *refined* tastes would appreciate a fine white one like yours and would be willin' to pay top dollar for it." He began easing up the blue poplin of Roxie's traveling skirt as he continued to nuzzle her ear and slobber into her blonde curls.

Roxie shifted her head away and took a long drag on the cigar. Garrison lifted a hand to boldly begin caressing one of her bosoms. "I'd be willing to act as your agent in Cimarron and arrange clients for you of the highest caliber."

I just bet you would and I'd never see a penny of anything you collected. Do you think I'm some green girl just off the stage who'd take up with any pimp? What a jackass.

"I'm on my way to Arizona, Mr. Garrison," Roxie said and stood unsteadily. She reached for the door sash to steady herself in the rocking coach as she moved to sit on the bench across from the annoying gambler, who seemed to think it was acceptable to take liberties with a lady simply because she'd practiced the Trade in the past.

"Of course, you are," he said with a slight sneer and shifted the cigar between his thin lips with his tongue. "You're a hard one, aren't ya? You don't show no gratitude to a gentleman who's just tryin' to do ya a good turn." He seated himself beside her again and reached into his vest pocket. He pulled out three silver dollars and held them up in front of Roxie's face. "I have money if you want me to be crass and offer to pay you for it."

"Most whores *do* get paid for it, sir," Roxie said with an irritated chuckle.

He dropped the coins into Roxie's lap. "Well, what can a fella get for three silvers? As you can see, I still use the real thing. I don't trust the paper scrip they're forcing on us from Washington." He took a deep breath and grinned over at her.

"Here?" she asked, wide-eyed. "Now?"

"Why not?" He said and shrugged his narrow shoulders. "Nobody in here but the two of us and we won't be in Cimarron for another three hours or so," he said with an expectant grin on his stubbled face. "Open that blouse, girlie. I want to get a mouthful of bosom." He yanked at Roxie's pale blue traveling skirt and she felt it sliding up over her silk petticoat. "And I want a handful of warm cunny too."

"You can get a feel and a taste," Roxie said as she scooped up the coins and dropped them into her bag with a satisfying clink. "But I'm not lettin' you between my legs in this damned bumpy coach." She unbuttoned her jacket and began fumbling with the pearl buttons to open her white silk blouse. "Pull out your cock and I'll suck it, but that's all you'll get in this damned coach for three dollars." Garrison frowned and Roxie heard him make a grumbling comment under his breath about greedy, ungrateful whores. "Take it or leave it, Mr. Garrison," she sighed. "It's of no consequence to me. Your damned money is in *my* bag now."

"Whores are whores," he mumbled, but began to fidget with the buttons on his worn, gray trousers.

Roxie smiled when he pulled out his small, semi-erect cock. He saw her grin and reached into her open blouse to shove a hand into her camisole and roughly pull a bosom up over the top of her tight corset. Before she could take a breath, he had a nipple between his teeth and began sucking and biting. Roxie rolled her eyes in amusement and leaned back. She pulled her skirts up to expose the pale skin of her thighs above her stockings and soon she felt Garrison's cold, smooth hand groping at her exposed crotch.

I'm glad I wore the crotchless bloomers after all. The bastard would likely have torn my good ones to get at it if I hadn't.

Garrison gave her nipple a hard bite and Roxie yelped. "You like that?" He asked and took another quick nip. She thought about slapping the side of the man's graying head, but simply gave a bored sigh and settled back.

He paid for it. Let him have his fun.

His fingers poked and prodded her cunny. His mouth released her nipple and he leered up at her.

"I think I want more than my cock sucked, whore. I paid you enough for three pokes." Roxie grabbed for purchase as Garrison yanked her around on the slick leather and pushed her head down against the leather upholstery. He maneuvered his body to straddle her hips on the narrow seat of the bouncing coach and Roxie blinked when his sweat dripped into her eye and down her cheek as he entered her and began pumping his tiny cock furiously into her cunny. "That's some right nice cunny," he panted. She didn't see any use in fighting the man. He'd paid, she'd let him play.

Garrison pumped and Roxie turned her head so she could stare off through the window at the occasional fluffy cloud in the bright blue autumn sky. She finally heard him gasp with his release and sag down atop her with all his weight. The scent of stale tobacco filled her nose from his greasy hair. Roxie lie there beneath him for a few long minutes before attempting to push him up and off her.

"OK, Hiram, you've had your fun. Get up off me so I can situate myself." When he didn't respond, Roxie grabbed a handful of limp gray curls and yanked his head up. She dropped it when she saw blank, dead eyes staring back at her from the face of Hiram Garrison.

Well, that's a first. I've never fucked one to death before. Mattie's surely gonna get a good laugh from this.

Roxie wriggled her petite frame out from beneath the dead weight of the gambler and sat up. She straightened her skirts, pushed her bosoms back into her camisole, and rebuttoned her blouse and jacket. Once she had herself situated, Roxie attended to the body of the late Hiram Garrison. She yanked his trousers up over his sagging white behind and pulled him up into a sitting position. His shriveled cock, she poked back into its place, and buttoned his trousers. Before leaning the dead man against the wall of the Butterfield Coach, Roxie riffled through his pockets to find his smokes and Lucifer's. She found two more silver dollars, but left those. She would not steal money from the dead. She left that for the undertaker in town.

When the coach pulled to a stop before the St. James Hotel in Cimarron, New Mexico, everyone was shocked by the blood-curdling scream that came from the poor woman riding in the coach when she realized the sleeping man she'd been riding with had actually been dead.

The good people at the St. James bought Roxie drinks and a meal and the coach's driver told her the line would cover the cost of her room that night. Roxie North went to bed after a hot bath in a very comfortable bed, well-fed and more than a little tipsy from the finest whiskey the St. James had to offer. The fine room, the bath, the supper, and the whiskey would have cost Roxie more than three dollars and she smiled as she settled under the quilt.

Thank you, Hiram Garrison. May you be passing through St. Peter's pearly gates before the devil knows you're dead.

Chapter 2

September 11, 1878

Mattie Kirby brushed tears from her red cheeks as she sliced ham at her kitchen counter to make a cold supper for her and her husband Joshua. It was only September, but the day had been blustery and cold with a light rain falling. They'd stood together as husband and wife while the preacher said the words over Emma Sue's little coffin before they laid her to rest in the church yard, but Joshua hadn't spoken.

He hadn't spoken more than a few words to her since Emma Sue had drawn her last breath two days before. Mattie had been helping Doc Robinson tend to folks suffering from the measles outbreak in Prescott. Mattie had served as the doctor's right hand since coming to town five months earlier from Colorado Springs. Her knowledge of herbal remedies, bone setting, and wound stitching had impressed the old doctor and he'd accepted her offer of assistance without hesitation.

Doc had assured Mattie that Emma Sue would be safe from the disease because nursing babies were immune to such things. Mattie had been shocked when her sweet baby woke up one early morning fussy and fevered. She'd run the four blocks to Doc's office with Emma Sue wrapped in a blanket after the first red rash erupted and her fever had soared. Doc had bathed Emma Sue with alcohol to ease the fever, but nothing had helped. She couldn't swallow and wouldn't nurse. The rash had broken out inside her little mouth and gone down her throat. Doc shook his head and told Mattie and Joshua he couldn't explain it.

"I don't know what to tell you folks," the white-headed doctor said as he scratched his stubbled chin. "All the books say a nursing infant should be immune to such infections, but this little one has about the worst case I've ever seen." He bathed the listless infant's forehead with a damp cloth while Mattie clung to her big husband.

"Will she get better, Doc?" Joshua asked as he shook Mattie off his arm and knelt by the narrow bed where his daughter lie, gasping for breath through tiny, dry, and cracked lips.

"I don't know, Joshua," the doctor replied. "We've been forcing fluids into her as best we can, but she won't take the breast and that's where she gets her nourishment from." He shook his old, white head. "I just don't know. This outbreak has claimed a dozen lives so far. It's particularly virulent."

Joshua Kirby had scooped up his infant daughter after she'd taken one last, long gasp and then gone silent and still on the white sheet. He'd hugged the baby to his breast as tears dripped into his bushy black beard. Mattie had wailed and tried to take the baby from him, but the big man had pushed her aside, returned the infant to the narrow bed and stormed out of the doctor's office without looking back at his grieving wife.

Mattie pushed a red curl behind her ear, remembering that horrible afternoon, and put the plates of cold sliced ham, yellow cheese, and yesterday's bread onto the round oak table. She was opening a jar of sweet pickles when she heard Joshua come into the room. She looked up to see her husband garbed in his traveling clothes, heavy jacket, wide-brimmed felt hat, and fur-lined gloves.

"Where are you going, Josh?" she muttered and sat the unopened jar of pickles onto the round oak table.

He dropped his bedroll onto the floor and kicked it. "Anywhere but here," he growled, glowering at his thin wife whose eyes were rimmed red from days of worry and weeping.

"What do you mean?" Mattie asked with her big, green eyes wide with dismay. His violent tone scared her some and she shivered.

"I'll not live under the same roof with a woman who'd kill her own child."

"Kill my own … what are you talking about, Joshua Kirby?" Mattie gasped, throwing her hand to cover her mouth.

"You went out tending to other folks' sick youngins and brought that disease back here to our little Emma Sue," he yelled, and shoved the table to send the delicate porcelain plates flying across the polished wood floor and shatter. The tall, husky man took a step toward his trembling, confused wife. "You killed our baby girl just the same as you'd put a knife through her little heart and I'll not live here with the likes of you, Matilda Grace." He kicked a coffee cup, bent, and picked up his tightly secured bedroll. "You can live here as long as you like," he said, motioning around the otherwise neat kitchen. "I'm going to join Will in Colorado. You can run the office until Jeramiah finds a replacement for me or you can go back to whorin'," he spat. "You're no fit woman to be neither a wife nor mother." Joshua stormed out the door, letting it slam loudly behind him.

Tears of rage and grief washed down Mattie's cheeks as she crumpled to the pine planks of the floor. She sobbed as she listened to the hooves of Joshua's big mare pound off across the yard and down the street.

He's leaving me. He's really leaving me. We just buried our baby girl and he's leaving me here alone. What am I going to do now?

Mattie sobbed on the floor until darkness fell and she had no more tears. With some effort she dragged herself to her feet and lit the wick of an oil lamp. Stiff from the chill, she opened the door to the firebox of the enameled iron cook-stove and used the poker to churn up the few red coals. Small blue flames spiked up and she pulled two split pieces of wood from the pile beside the stove and tossed them onto the empty firebox. Mattie blew her nose on the soggy handkerchief she pulled from her skirt pocket as she trudged into the parlor to add some wood to the potbelly there, as well. She heard heavy raindrops pelting the roof. It would be a cold, damp night and she'd be spending it alone for the first time since arriving in Prescott.

She peered sadly around her parlor, remembering the day she'd hung the flowered curtains with their lace trim and how proud she'd been when she and Joshua had first sat together on the long velvet settee with its matching wingback chairs and ottoman. She'd been afraid Josh's big body and her pregnant one might break the delicate furniture, but it hadn't and they'd laughed together over it. It had only been a few months ago, but it seemed like a lifetime ago now.

After feeding the fires and lighting another lamp, Mattie returned to the kitchen and cleaned up the mess on the floor. Her heart ached as she picked up pieces of her broken china. She remembered how proud she'd been to display the pieces in her hutch when Joshua had surprised her with it after they'd moved into the house he'd built for her and their expected child.

It wasn't a big house, but it was cozy with two bedrooms, a kitchen with a pantry, and a parlor. Joshua had painted the clapboard siding a buttery yellow and the window trim and porch posts bright white. Her saved money from what she'd earned in the Trade had paid for the land and the materials, but legally the house belonged to Joshua. She lived there at his pleasure, but she hadn't cared about such legalities. The handsome little house was theirs. The attic offered room to expand when other children arrived, Joshua had told her and she'd been so happy when they'd bought furniture from local carpenters and Riley's Mercantile. Mattie had spent hours sewing curtains and braiding rugs. She finally had a house of her own with a husband she loved and a child on the way. What woman could want for more?

Now she'd lost her baby along with her husband. She swept up the last of the shattered china and went to her desk for paper and pen. She set the lamp on the kitchen table to give her light and wrote to both her sister Miriam and her best friend Roxie. She told them both about Emma Sue's passing, but only wrote to Roxie about Joshua's leaving and his terrible accusations.

How can he blame me, Rox? Doc swore Emma Sue would be immune to the measles. I never would have gone into any sick houses if I'd thought I might bring it home and make my baby sick. Doc said it would be safe.

As she brushed out her red curls before braiding them for sleep, Mattie listened for the sound of his horse and Joshua's return. She hoped he'd ride in the rain and then realize what a mistake he'd made and turn around. No hoof beats came in the night, however, and Mattie fell into a restless sleep, tossing and turning with Joshua's face twisted in anger calling her a murdering whore. Lightening flashed and thunder rolled across the mountains, intruding into Mattie's dreams. As it grew colder, the heavy, beating rain turned to pinging, icy sleet and then to soft, silent snow.

Cold permeated the little house and Mattie wrapped herself in her velvet dressing gown before padding barefoot to add more wood to the fires in the parlor stove and the kitchen. Joshua had not returned and more tears leaked from her eyes as she pumped water into the coffee pot. She drank two cups of strong, hot coffee, but it didn't warm her.

Mattie dressed in a black suit and mourning bonnet. It was business-like, but reflected her state of mourning, as she walked through the icy mud into town to post her letters. She then trudged up the muddy street to open the office of Harvey and Edwards Mining, where she had assisted Joshua and attended to the purchasing of supplies and equipment for the company's Arizona concerns.

Joshua Kirby actually held the title of purchasing agent because he was the man, but everyone knew Mattie Kirby actually ran the office. Men in the mining business felt more at ease thinking they dealt with another man, but nothing got a stamp of approval unless Mrs. Kirby gave it her nod. Joshua made trips to the outlying mines and discussed things with operators and engineers. He took their requests in writing and brought them back to Mattie who went over them and checked prices with suppliers before making any purchases on the company's behalf. Suppliers came to Prescott to wine and dine Joshua Kirby, but it soon came to be known that it was Mrs. Kirby's influence they needed to garner.

"Good morning, Mrs. Kirby," said Emmet Grady, the town's telegrapher. as they passed on the boardwalk. "Me and the Mrs. were really sorry to hear about the passing of your little one, ma'am."

"Thank you, Mr. Grady. Please pass my thanks on to your kind wife, as well."

"I'll do that," he said and tipped his cap. "If there's anything we can do for you or Mr. Kirby let me know." He looked up and down the street. "Will Mr. Kirby be along? You usually open up the office together."

Mattie cleared her throat. "Mr. Kirby was called away to Colorado on urgent company business."

Mattie saw him raise an eyebrow and knew the man would know she'd lied. If Joshua had been called away, Mr. Grady would have seen the telegram. The man was the biggest gossip in Prescott and spread news faster than a women's sewing circle. She didn't wait for his reply and pushed past the pasty-faced man in his blue company suit.

Lord only knows what tales he'll be spreading around town about Joshua's leaving. I hated to ask, but I hope Roxie comes. It's such a very long way from Dodge, though.

Chapter 3

November 20, 1878

Roxie had been traveling for almost four weeks and was more than ready to be done with it. The long days of bouncing around in the stage annoyed her and sleeping in dirty rooms or on pallets on dirt floors with mice running across her blankets had Roxie at her wits end. Towns had been few and far between once they'd left Cimarron. Albuquerque had been the only town of any size and the only place they'd stopped with a real hotel with beds. They had spent most nights at small stage stops peopled by Indians or dusky-skinned, dark-eyed Mexicans.

She'd been jolted awake in the night more than once by the braying of sheep in their pens, made restless by the loud yipping of packs of coyotes nearby. They'd seen few white settlements along their way and Roxie had eaten her fill of black beans, spicy peppers, stringy goat meat, and ground corn tortillas. Her mouth watered for the taste of crispy fried chicken, mashed potatoes and warm, buttered biscuits.

Today they would be stopping at a lonely army post where the men scouted for and guarded against marauding Indians, but Roxie didn't anticipate much in the way of comfort there. At other posts where they'd stopped, they'd been relegated to the civilian camps built up around them populated by tame Indians, itinerant gamblers, and whores of the lowest order who serviced them and the military men.

Roxie supposed she could have been one of those whores had her friend Sue not relocated from Fort Dodge to Abilene when she had.

Roxie and Mattie had been on their way to join her there when she'd sent word to St. Louis about the change in plans. Roxie shivered thinking about the dirty, used-up women at the military posts and thanked Sue where ever she might be for that move from Fort Dodge to Abilene back in 1870. The city of Dodge hadn't existed then and Sue and her girls had been working in shabby tents set up outside the walls of Fort Dodge. Roxie and Mattie had ended up in cribs in Abilene, but with clean beds, wooden floors, solid rooves, and bathtubs. Poor Sue, however, had succumbed to consumption not long after their arrival in Abilene. Roxie doubted the women in these military camps bathed more than once or twice a year and suspected lice crawled over their beds and bodies.

Roxie involuntarily scratched at her powder-blonde head, thinking about lice as the coach came to a stop on a dusty lane in front of a brown, sunbaked adobe building with a covered porch. She heard guitar music and laughter coming from inside as she and another woman stepped down from the coach. Roxie used her kerchief to wipe her face and scowled when the cloth came away brown with sweat and travel dust.

"I'll see to your bags getting to your rooms, ladies," the sunburned driver told them. "Mrs. Marcus your bags will be taken to the married officers' quarters where your husband resides and your bags," he said over his shoulder to Roxie, "will be taken to one of the guest rooms in the back of this cantina."

Roxie rolled her eyes and hoped this guest room came with an actual bed and a door with a keyed lock. She climbed the stairs and walked into the noisy common room where three Mexican men played guitars and sang in Spanish while a girl with long black hair and dusky skin danced in a swirling red dress.

Juliet Marcus, Roxie's traveling companion since their stop in Albuquerque, was a new bride and traveling to join her husband at this post from Fort Smith, Arkansas. The young bride was only twenty-two and quite innocent. Roxie had enjoyed the girl's company, nonetheless, with her endless chatter about the latest fashions and hairstyles. They'd exchanged copies of periodicals with bright color plates to study along the way.

"Thank you, sir," Juliet said as they stepped out of the coach. She looked up and down the dusty street then grabbed Roxie by the sleeve. "Oh my gracious, Roxanna, will you look at that?" She nodded to a group of men and women walking toward the stage.

"What?" Roxie asked gazing at the women arm-in-arm with uniformed men she suspected were their husbands.

"Why, my momma was wearin' clothes cut like that *before* the war," the girl gasped.

Roxie grinned at the hooped skirts and wide sleeves on the clean, but out of date dresses the women wore. "Women's fashions change," Roxie quipped, "but military uniforms stay the same."

"And look at their hair," the girl said wide-eyed. "Those long danglin' curls have been out of style for ten years at least."

"I don't suppose they get many hairstylists this far away from the cities," Roxie said, suppressing a grin at the young woman's obvious distress.

"How old do you think those women are Roxanna? Surely they're those boy's mommas and not their *wives.* They all look so *old.*"

Roxie had noted the same about women throughout her travels. The uncivilized west seemed to age women more so than men. The group walked by and the intimate hand holding and eye-batting convinced Roxie these were married couples and not mothers and sons. The horrified look on Juliet's young face and the tears welling in her eyes let Roxie know the girl had been convinced of the same.

"Oh my gracious, Roxanna," Juliet wailed. "We're supposed to be posted here for five *years*. William wants to be a career military man like his father and that means being posted in the west. Do you think *I'm* gonna look that old and out of style when *we* get reposted?"

Roxie suddenly felt sorry for the innocent young woman at her side. She stared after the group who'd passed them by, knowing what awaited Juliet. Her freshness and her innocence would fade. Her face, her hair, and her clothes would age. The world far away from the western military encampments would change, but isolated as she would be, Juliet would leave this post in five years looking ten years older and wearing terribly outdated fashions.

"Not if you keep up with the periodicals," Roxie said, taking the girl's trembling hands. "You said you're a good seamstress. Watch the periodicals and simply re-fit your existing wardrobe to the new styles."

"Do you really think so?"

"I know so," Roxie said and patted the girl's trembling, gloved hand. "My friend Mattie redid lots of our clothes when new styles came along and we couldn't afford to buy new ones. She even made a little extra money redoin' our friends' clothes, too."

The girl's eyes went wide and a smile creased her dusty face. "I could do that. A military man doesn't make much money, you know. William would appreciate any extra income I might be able to generate."

"There you go," Roxie sighed and smiled at the girl. "If they don't have a seamstress here at the fort maybe you could open a little shop or work out of your quarters."

"What an absolutely stupendous idea," Juliet said enthusiastically as a young officer walked up and took her into his arms.

"What's a stupendous idea?" he asked as he whirled Juliet around and planted a kiss upon her soft, pink lips.

Roxie left the young lovers to their reintroduction, hugged her bag to her midsection, and stepped up onto the covered porch of the noisy cantina. A blue haze of tobacco smoke wafted out of the open door as she entered and Roxie held her kerchief to her nose against the smell of unwashed bodies, tobacco, and stale alcohol.

A few men in military uniforms slouched on benches, drinking, smoking, and leering at the dancer's bare shoulders and ankles. A few turned their heads as the pretty, petite blonde entered the room to register for her night's stay.

"Now there's a good lookin' woman," one of them yelled. "Come on over here and let us buy you a drink, honey. We don't see many pretty, white women way out here."

Roxie ignored the soldier's crude remarks and continued signing the book to register for her room. She followed the fat barman's directions and passed through the noisy cantina past the leering, grasping military men, the dancing girl, and the musicians. Roxie passed through a door and out into a courtyard shaded by feathery-leafed trees and saw rows of doors made from rough-cut lumber painted bright blue and red that marked the rooms for the visitors to the dusty, military outpost.

Roxie found the door with number seven painted upon it and opened it to find a narrow cot high off the floor with what looked like a comfortable thick mattress, overstuffed pillow, and brightly patched quilt. She smiled when she saw a washstand with an enameled bowl and pitcher standing next to the bed. A large crack marred the oval mirror above the washstand and Roxie sighed at her dingy, disheveled reflection.

What I wouldn't give for a hot bath. I surely hope Mattie has a tub in that house of hers.

She peeked into the pitcher and smiled when she saw it contained clean water almost up to the spout. Her bags had been stacked

20

at the foot of the narrow bed on the packed dirt floor. She'd spent so many nights in rooms like this and it eased her mind that she wouldn't be on the floor. With a long, tired sigh, Roxie turned the brass key and locked the door.

At least I have a bed up off the floor and I'll be able to wash off some of this dust. I haven't been able to properly wash my hair in over a week.

She lifted her heaviest leather case onto the bed and unbuckled the straps. Roxie rummaged through her things until she found a simple sleeveless night dress and her velvet dressing gown. She'd eaten a plate of spicy beans at their lunch stop and didn't plan to go into the noisy cantina for a supper of the same. She had rock candy in her bag and whiskey in her flask. She tested the firm mattress and smiled.

A good wash and a long rest is what I need more than greasy beans and goat cheese.

Roxie poured some of the tepid water into the bowl. Not hot, but it would have to do. She stripped out of her poplin traveling suit and shook it before hanging it on a hook at the end of the bed. Her camisole and petticoat she tossed alongside the case. First she tended to her hair, pouring some of the cool water over her head to wet it. She lathered her hair with a goodly amount of her precious lavender soap. Thus far it had kept the lice away. Scratching her scalp as she worked in the lather felt good. She dipped her wet, blonde locks into the bowl before pouring the remainder of the pitcher's contents over her head for a thorough rinse.

After wringing the water from her thick, blonde curls and wrapping her head in a cotton towel from her bag, Roxie lathered a washcloth with the lavender soap and scrubbed her face, arms, privates, and finally her tired feet. She shivered in the chilly room, but it felt good to be clean. She wriggled into her night dress and wrapped her dressing gown around her damp body before shaking out her hair and tending to the tangles with her silver comb.

As she ran the teeth through one last time, Roxie heard a knock at her door.

"It's the driver, miss," an unfamiliar male voice called from outside, "we've had some trouble with the horses necessitating a change in the schedule. Can you open up so I can talk to ya about it?"

Roxie rolled her eyes in agitation as she turned the brass key in the lock and cracked the door to peek out at the man. "I'm not really dressed for company," she said as the door pushed open, knocking her back into the room and onto the floor beside the bed. "What the hell," Roxie gasped and looked up to see two men in blue uniforms barrel into the little room and quickly shut the door behind them.

"I told ya it was her," said a wiry, little man of about forty with a scruffy beard and dirty blonde hair cut short around his big ears. "She's a whore from Dodge City who worked in them cribs down by the tracks." He licked his lips and leered down at Roxie who struggled with the quilt, trying to pull herself up off the dirt floor.

"Looks like we can have us some sweet white cunny tonight, Danny boy," he said in a thick Irish accent and punched the larger man on the shoulder. "I'm sick to death of smelly Mex cunny. Ain't you?"

The big man reached down as if to offer Roxie his hand, but grabbed a handful of damp hair instead and yanked hard. "I want 'er first," he sneered and pulled Roxie up to shove her onto the narrow bed. "Why don't you go see if Kutter and a few of the other fellas want a taste? We can charge 'em a dollar each at the door. When word gets around 'bout what we got here we could make us a tidy little sum before the mornin'."

The skinny man stared at Roxie cowering on the bed and smiled. "Tis a grand idea, Danny me boy, but I want me cock drained in 'er before dem others get at 'er." He took a step toward the bed past his big uniformed friend. "Tis only fittin' 'tis as I'm the one brought 'er to your attention and all, Danny Boy."

The big man pushed his friend back toward the door. "I'll have the first taste," he growled, "I'm your superior officer." Dan turned back toward the little man. "Now go get Kutter and his crew." He unbuckled his belt and began releasing the buttons on his blue military trousers. "This little whore is gonna suck me dry then she's gonna make us some real money here tonight."

"Oh, Danny boy," the little man whined, "if ye're gonna take her mouth, den let me pump her cunny full. I got me a load here dat's just achin' to be let out." He brushed his hand over the bulge in his dusty blue trousers.

"No," snapped the big officer. "I prefer having my fun in private. You go on and I'll let you fill her cunny before Kutter and the others get at her. Kutter may want her slicked up first, anyhow, the man said with a chuckle and squeezed his crotch. He's got a big cock."

"Oh, alright," sighed the man, looking beaten with his eyes downcast, "but don't be damagin' her overmuch. I know what sorta *fun* ye like to be havin' with the women ye play with."

The door slammed and Roxie found herself alone with the leering hulk of bluebelly. She hadn't been idle while the two stood conversing, however. Her velvet handbag that had been hanging from the headboard post now lay tucked up under the stout feather pillow in easy reach.

Roxie sat quietly as the big man opened his trousers, reached in and pulled out his stiff, thick cock. He fondled it lovingly. "Now, bitch," he growled as he reached for Roxie, "I like a woman to beg me for this." He shook the organ. "You bein' a whore, you ought to be accustomed to such requests, but I want it to sound natural like." He grabbed Roxie's hair and tugged her head toward his crotch. "Beg me to fill your mouth and I'll not choke you overmuch with it," he said and chuckled grimly, but pulled her head up to stare into his leering face. "And don't you dare think about biting me, bitch, or you'll get the same thing I gave the last little biter."

"What? A mouth full of blood?" Roxie sneered.

He tugged Roxie's head savagely, but she refused to utter a whimper of pain. She knew men like him got their pleasure from seeing and hearing a woman in pain. Charles Devaroe's handsome face suddenly came to mind and Roxie had to push the abusive owner of the riverboat *The Ruby Queen* from her mind. She wouldn't give this big bluebelly the fun of thinking he'd caused her any pain or fear.

"No," he said and pushed Roxie back onto the narrow bed where he yanked at her night dress and pulled out a bosom, pinching and twisting her nipple. "I bit the bitch's nipples off and spit them in her face while her wailing brats looked on."

"So much for military honor," Roxie spat, "bluebelly scum."

He backhanded her and Roxie saw stars before her eyes and tasted the coppery flavor of blood in her mouth. "William there said you were a Reb bitch, but he's Irish and has a difficult time with accents." He straddled Roxie and began inching his cock up toward her face. "Reb or Union," he snarled, "makes no matter. You're a woman and you're in sore need of being taught to mind a man." He slapped her hard again. "William's right, though. We haven't had any white cunny in a damned long time out here." He got a far off look in his eyes and a smile cracked his broad, clean-shaven face. "As a matter of fact that little Mormon biter was the last bit of white cunny I tasted before bein' sent down here to deal with these Arizona red-skins." He settled his weight across Roxie's mid-section as he mused and twisted one nipple and then the other.

"We'd just cleaned up a mess of Shoshone and were headed south to find some more when we came upon this little homestead," he mused. "First we thought they'd been wiped out because the barn was all burned, but here comes this sweet little thing out on the porch with a babe in arms and another almost bleedin' age hangin' onto her skirts." He smiled down at Roxie. "She had a boy, too, as I recall, but no grown man about. Me and the boys were all worked up after the raid and in need of a little relief, you understand." He shook his head and smiled as he stroked his cock with more vigor.

"The little bitch should have been grateful to the U.S. Army for protecting her and her brats from those savages and given us our due, but she put up a hell of a fuss." He stroked his hard cock, remembering and Roxie saw it begin to ooze. "She offered us coffee," he sneered, "but got all high and mighty when one of the boys put a hand on the younger cunny's behind." He began to stroke faster. "I would have liked to have popped that one myself, but some of the others dragged her out and had at her and … the boy too, I'm thinking," he sniggered. "I could hear the squealing as the boys took 'em and the bitch's beggin' were pleasin' beyond belief." His eyes rolled up into his head and the hand moved faster on his stiff tool.

He recognized the disgust on Roxie's face and frowned. "They was just filthy, Mormon scum. Everyone knows Mormons are perverted creatures and enjoy bein' used in every way. They try to use the Good Book as justification for their perversions and that little bitch should have just given us our due when we asked for it." He stroked faster. "I made her beg for it and she begged real nice," he groaned as he shot his release across Roxie's bare breasts. He appeared to have lost interest in Roxie's mouth as he lost himself in his depraved memories. "You should have heard that little bitch beg when we herded them all down into that cellar with our rifles on our shoulders."

He began to laugh as he rubbed his juice onto her breasts. He never noticed Roxie's eyes widen as recognition about something in his ravings jogged her memory.

Naomi and the children. This bastard is talking about Naomi and her children. It was him and his bluebelly friends who killed her and those poor babies up there in Utah.

Anger blazed in Roxie's cheeks when she realized this bastard had been responsible for doing so much more than just killing the poor young woman and her family. Roxie snaked her hand up under the pillow and found her velvet drawstring bag.

"Get off me you bluebelly bastard," Roxie yelled and rolled with strength she didn't know she possessed.

The big man lost his balance and tumbled off the bed, his arms flailed about and he grabbed at Roxie's bare legs to keep from landing on the floor.

Roxie gave his crotch a hard kick when his weight lifted off her. "You're a sickening son-of-a-bitch," she continued and swung her arm up with her Derringer clutched in her white-knuckled fist. "That was a good woman and innocent children you abused and murdered."

"What the hell," he howled as he stood. Red rage etched Bluebelly Dan's face and he lunged toward the bed with his big fists clenched. "I'm gonna beat you to death you filthy, little Reb whore."

His eyes went wide when Roxie fired both barrels of her Derringer into his wilted, naked crotch. He fell to the floor screaming and clutching at the bloody spot between his thighs where his cock and ballocks hung in bloody, ruined tatters.

Roxie jumped from the bed and rushed to the door, clutching at her torn night dress. Her velvet dressing gown hung open. She yanked the door open and screamed, "Help me! Somebody help me, please."

People came rushing from the cantina at the sound of Roxie's piercing screams. The dancing girl in her red ruffled dress rushed to take a disheveled blonde into her arms. "What has happened *senorita?*"

"Men came to my door," Roxie sobbed and pointed to the open door of room number seven. "One of them said he was the stage driver and needed to talk to me," Roxie hiccupped through tears. "But they were soldiers and …" she choked, shivering in the cold, night air. "They said they were going to sell me to the other soldiers," she cried, clinging to the dusky-skinned young woman. Roxie scanned the gathered onlookers to see the skinny soldier in the crowd and pointed. "He's the other one. He was supposed to go out and find somebody called Kutter and bring him and his friends back to … to sell me to."

Roxie slumped in the girl's arms as an older man with officer's braids pushed through the murmuring crowd.

"What's going on out here, Rosa?" He asked the dancer cradling the petite blonde in her arms.

"Your *puercos* have gone too far this time, Major." She pointed to the cowering William. "He and his dog friend have broken into the room of one of my customers from the stage and savagely assaulted her." She gently turned Roxie's face toward the Major so he could see the bruises that had begun to rise on her pale skin and her swollen bloody lips. "I have complained of them to you before, but when they assault my brown-skinned women you do nothing. What will you do now that they've attacked a pretty white woman who is a customer of the stage line and not a simple girl from the camp?"

A soldier came rushing up and said breathless, "Dan … Lieutenant Russell … He's in her room and he's been shot … in his privates, sir. She shot him in his privates. He's dead, sir," the soldier said pointing a trembling finger at Roxie. "She murdered him."

"She's a whore from Dodge City," William yelled, stepping forward, confidently, for the first time. "I know 'er from the cribs dere when I was stationed at Fort Dodge, sir. She tis but a dirty, murderin' whore." He cleared his throat and stood stiffly before the Major. "She recognized me in de saloon and asked me an' Danny Boy … Lieutenant

Russell to hustler her up some business for de night." He glared down at Roxie. "She said she'd service me and de Lieutenant fer free if we would. He sent me off to see to it while he took 'is turn wid 'er first, ya see."

The Major ran a hand through his white hair and sighed. "Miss I'm gonna need you to come to Rosa's office to clear this up. Rosa can come with you if you'd like, but we need to talk." He looked away as Roxie pulled her dressing gown up to cover her torn night dress. "Would you like to go back to your room and change first?"

Roxie turned to take a quick look at the door to her room that now stood open with uniformed men milling about inside and out.

"I don't want to go back in there … not while that terrible beast is in there," she wailed, shaking her head with her blonde waves falling into her big tear-filled, blue eyes.

"Alright, alright," the Major said, attempting to calm Roxie. "Rosa will you help the young lady to your office? Private," he growled at William, "you come with me, as well."

"*Si,* Major," Rosa said and began pulling Roxie to her feet. "Is he telling the truth?" she asked Roxie softly. "Are you a *punta* from this Dodge City?"

Roxie turned to the woman she now saw was older than she'd first thought. "It's true that I once practiced the Trade in Dodge City, but that was some time ago. I'm just a woman traveling alone to visit my friend in Arizona now and I don't know that man." She nodded toward the private.

They walked through the courtyard past staring soldiers and into the cantina where they passed the bar and entered a small room with a desk and two ladder-back chairs. The Major stood behind one, and waited until the women entered. William stood against the wall with his shoulders slumped and his eyes downcast. Rosa took the chair behind her desk and Roxie took the other in front of it. The Major held it for her as she sat.

"Now young lady," the Major said, "we need to get this mess cleared up. Do you know this man, Private Mulroney, from Dodge City?" He motioned his head toward the skinny soldier.

"I can't say that I know him, Major, but he didn't lie when he said that I worked in the Dodge City cribs," Roxie admitted in a hushed tone. "However, I haven't practiced the Trade for some time. You can wire Dodge and verify that with Bat Masterson, Ford County sheriff."

"You didn't make propositions to my men in this cantina?"

"She did not talk to them in my cantina," Rosa cut in. "They spoke to her with much rudeness, but she ignored them and walked away to her room. You can ask Marco and the other players. They saw it all."

"She motioned to us … from out in the courtyard and … we talked to her there," Mulroney stammered.

"The *puercos* did not leave the cantina until an hour after dark, Major," Rosa said resolutely glaring at the private. "He lies."

"Private," the Major growled, "I suggest you remain silent until I've heard what the young lady has to say."

"Yes, sir, but keep in mind dat she's an admitted whore and whores dey be natural liars." Mulroney said boldly.

"Quiet, private," the Major snapped. "Now miss, please tell us what happened in your room tonight. I know it might be uncomfortable, but I need to hear your side of this story for my report."

Roxie spent the next half hour relating the evening's events with tears and sobs. She watched Mulroney roll his eyes at her theatrics, but keep he managed to keep his comments to himself while she spoke.

"Major," Roxie added, "the man in my room made admissions to me about the murders of a young woman and her family last year in the Utah territory. I don't know if this man was involved," Roxie said, nodding toward the cowering Irishman, "but he told me the one called Kutter was along with other men in his troop. My husband and I found the bodies of the poor woman and her children in their cellar. It was horrible," Roxie sobbed. "They shot babies and a woman who did nothing but defend the honor of her young daughter and refuse their lecherous advances. Will you investigate this … this dishonorable atrocity?"

The Major turned to Mulroney. "What do you know about this, Private? Didn't you arrive here at the same time and from the same unit as Sargent Kutter and the Lieutenant?"

"I didn't join the unit until after the raids up in Utah, Major. As for Danny Boy … the Lieutenant … murderin' women and children, I got no knowledge of any such happenings, but she's right when she says Kutter was with the Lieutenant up there. He might know about it."

"Get Kutter to my office," the Major yelled to the soldiers standing outside the door. "Miss, you have my word as an officer and a gentleman that these accusations will be investigated to the best of my ability and this … *man*," he nodded toward Mulroney, "will be dealt with. I'm sorry this happened to you on my post and I hope you won't hold it against the entire U.S. Army."

Roxie stood and extended her hand. "Of course not, major, and thank you ever so much for your kindness."

"Rosa, will you see to the lady's things being moved to another room? Just send the bill for it and any damages in the other room to my quartermaster and I'll see it's paid."

"Why thank you ever so much, Major," Roxie said in her sweetest southern drawl. "That beast pushed me and when my head hit," Roxie said and rubbed the side of her head gently, "it put a terrible crack in that lovely mirror over the washstand." She winked at Rosa, who gave her a grateful smile in return.

Chapter 4

December 11, 1878

Mattie sat nervously in the lobby of the Palace Hotel in one of the plush wingback chairs as she waited for the three o'clock stage to arrive in Prescott from Williams. Roxie had telegraphed Mattie from Albuquerque, New Mexico, informing her that the stage would arrive in Prescott on today's date at three in the afternoon. That had been almost a month ago, however, and she hadn't had further word from her friend.

The man at the counter had assured her the stage would be on time or within an hour and that he hadn't had any word about any delays regarding a Mrs. Roxanna Edwards or North. Mattie wasn't certain which name Roxie had decided to use since her divorce from Willard Edwards.

I'd bet she's using Edwards as a married woman traveling alone would garner less scrutiny than an unmarried one. Rox is smart that way. I'm sure she's using Edwards even if it chaps her hide to do so. Willard Edwards and Joshua Kirby deserve one another. I hope they're keeping each other warm at night in the cold Rocky Mountains this winter.

Snow had fallen a few times in Prescott that winter, but as Mattie had come to know, it only stayed on the ground for a few days before the warm Arizona sun melted it away, leaving a sea of mud in its wake. The ground hadn't frozen solid at all and most of the fields and her yard had greens sprouting beneath the browned winter grasses. This would be her first winter in Arizona and was proving to be an interesting one. She'd never lived any place where winters were quite so warm.

Mattie had spent the past weeks cleaning her house in anticipation of Roxie's arrival. She'd scrubbed floors, beaten rugs, and rearranged her furniture in the parlor a dozen times. It had broken her heart, but she'd finally cleaned out Emma Sue's room and done away with her things, replacing the infant's furniture with a new adult-sized bed and wardrobe from the mercantile.

The toys and clothes, she'd packed up and taken to the foundling home where Mattie knew the Trade girls in town took their unwanted babies. With the many mines in the area, Fort Whipple full of soldiers, and the fact that it housed the territorial capital, Prescott had a brisk Trade. High end girls worked out of The Palace Hotel, while cribs lined a whole street downtown. In her capacity as Doc Robinson's assistant, Mattie had attended upon the births of many of those children.

Midwifing had become one of her main duties along with traveling around the area tending wounds and broken bones the doctor had initially seen to. Mattie had become the old doctor's stand-in and many around Prescott now came directly to her for minor concerns rather than bothering the doctor at his office. Mattie suspected the fact that she didn't ask to be paid for her services contributed some to that as well. It had still worried Mattie, however, that she was taking his business.

"Dear Lord, girl. I've got no time for scraped knees and runny noses," the doctor had laughed when Mattie had apologized, worried he'd be upset with her for taking his paying patients from him. "If you don't mind dealing with Tilly Hammond every time one of her brood comes down with a sniffle or her when she comes up pregnant with another, you're welcome to her. She hasn't paid me a copper penny for my services in over a year. What about you?"

"She brought me a jar of apple butter and some eggs last month," Mattie said with an embarrassed giggle.

"You're doing better than me, then," Doc said with a smile and patted Mattie's arm. "How are you doing over there all alone, Mattie? Are you getting by? Do you need any help around the place now that Joshua's gone?"

"I'm doing alright, Doc," Mattie had sighed, "Mrs. Hammond's oldest boy, Jessie, comes over and chops firewood for me and has promised to come plow the garden in the spring. I think I can count on him for the heavy chores and he and his Poppa bring me game when they have extra. They brought me the hind quarter of an elk they took down just last week and hung it in the smokehouse. With what Joshua left, I think I'm in good shape for the winter," she said sadly.

Doc shook his head. "I'll never understand that husband of yours running off and leaving you like he did." Doc took Mattie's hands in his. "I blame myself for what happened. If I hadn't been relying on you so heavily during that measles outbreak, Emma Sue might still be alive and you'd still have a husband to care for your needs."

"Don't fret over it, Doc," Mattie sighed. "It was Emma Sue's time. For whatever reason, God wanted her back with him. I suppose he needed her more than he thought I did." Mattie shrugged her shoulders and took a deep breath. "I have to think of it that way, Doc, or I'd have gone mad with grief. Joshua went a little mad, I think. He couldn't find it in his way of thinking to blame God, so he blamed me." She brushed away a tear. "I'm going to be alright, Doc. My very best friend, Roxie Edwards, is coming all the way from Dodge City to stay with me."

Mattie was thinking about that conversation when she heard a familiar voice and turned in her chair to see a stylishly dressed, statuesque brunette coming down the wide oak stairs beside a tall, pale man in a stylishly cut, black silk suit. Mattie stood and took a step toward the stairs.

"Katie?" she said firmly to get the woman's attention.

The woman's big brown eyes lit up and a smile spread across the pretty face. "Mattie Wallace? Is this really you?" Kate Horony or Big-Nose Katie Elder, as she was sometimes called, lifted her green silk skirt and skipped down the stairs to fly into Mattie's outstretched arms. "Oh my God, it *is* you. Our Roxanna told me you had moved to this Arizona Territory," Kate said in her Hungarian accented voice, "but I had no idea you were here in *this* town. What a happy surprise. You surely aren't working from this place." Katie motioned around the lushly furnished lobby of the Palace Hotel. "Roxanna said you'd married and had a child."

"Had," Mattie huffed. "My baby died of the measles this past September and Joshua left me. He's off somewhere in Colorado with Roxie's man."

Katie shook her beautifully coifed head. "Men! They are all just pigs. You and Roxanna are both better off without them."

"Now, Darlin'," the well-dressed man from the stairs said in a voice with a deep southern drawl, reminding Mattie of Roxie's, "if I didn't know you better, I'd take offence at that remark."

Kate turned to the man and smiled. "Not you, of course, my love. You are a true gentleman of the highest quality." She turned to Mattie. "Mattie this is my companion Doctor John Holliday. We are on our way south to join Wyatt and his brothers. Morgan has taken the position as Marshall in the mining town Tombstone. Do you know it?"

"Indeed, I do," she replied. "Harvey and Edwards has a silver claim there and some copper claims nearby in Globe." Mattie allowed the doctor to take her hand and kiss her knuckles with his cold, bluish lips. She noted a sheen of perspiration on his brow, though the lobby of the Palace was quite cool. His hand felt clammy in hers, as well.

He has the look of illness about him. I wonder if he's contracted something from a patient. I hope Katie knows what it is. She seems quite smitten with him. I wonder if this is the drunken, gambling, dentist Roxie said Katie met when she went down to Texas.

"Will you be opening a practice in Tombstone, Doctor?" Mattie asked as she returned to her seat. "If their mining community is anything like the one here, they can't have too many doctors in attendance. Poor Doc Robinson here in Prescott is covered up with injured miners."

"I'm afraid my specialty is dentistry, my dear, and not the setting of broken bones, but yes, I plan to hang a shingle when we reach the lovely Tombstone and tend to the aching jaws there."

"You mean if Morgan and Wyatt allow you time to pursue your own endeavors," Katie snarled.

"Now, my dear, you know I've promised the brothers Earp my assistance when they have need of it." He patted her hand affectionately. "You and I shall have more than ample time to build a life of our own there."

"I'll believe that when I see it," Kate huffed and sat in one of the other wingback chairs.

"Have you lost your appreciation for Wyatt and his brothers?" Mattie asked with a sly grin.

"Why, I never knew you *had* an appreciation for my dear friend Wyatt and his family, Katherine," he quipped. "Your friend will have to enlighten me."

"I've never been fond of Wyatt Earp and his brothers," Mattie said solemnly. "Katie spent her time at the Long Branch while in Dodge and my friend Roxie and I spent our time at the Lady Gay with Jimmy Masterson. Is Wyatt still bedding that little drug addled Mattie Blaylock?"

"He certainly is. She tells everyone they're married, but I know he never took her before a minister," Kate said smugly. "And James went and took up with Miss Bessie. She even sold her lovely House in Dodge to fund and travel with him to this Tombstone. It seems all the Dodge City whores have turned a new leaf and play at being respectable now with husbands in Arizona."

"Now, my darling, Katherine," Doc said with a smile beneath his neatly trimmed mustache, "any intelligent man knows an experienced woman is the only woman worth wedding and bedding." He winked at Mattie and swatted Katie's behind playfully.

"Because he knows she can always make a living for both of them if necessary," Katie mumbled under her breath. "Do you see Virgil here in town, Mattie? We had dinner with him and lovely Allie at their home with Wyatt and Morgan. He's the one who convinced the brothers to give up on Dodge and travel to Arizona. He's all for giving up his job at the sawmill here and joining his brothers in the mining business down in Tombstone, but Allie would rather stay up here out of the heat. She thinks Wyatt is too quick tempered and will get them all killed." Kate gave Holliday a quick glance and looked away.

"I read in the paper that he was a constable here, but I haven't had any call to go visiting," Mattie said smugly. "I doubt Allie Earp would be open much to having *another* former whore sittin' in her fine parlor."

"Miss Allie is a fine woman," Doc interjected, "I'm certain she would be as gracious to you in her lovely home as she was to Katherine and I."

The big grandfather clock chimed three and Mattie glanced toward the tall glass-paned doors. "Roxie's coming in on the three o'clock stage, Katie. She's going to be so thrilled to see you here."

A broad smile creased the brunette's face. "Is this true, Mattie? She was still in Dodge when we departed, but we had to attend to some business matters down in Texas before coming west and left Dodge in July. We are here in Prescott because Wyatt had to file some claim paperwork here in the Capital before going on to Tombstone."

"Miss Roxanna is a truly delightful creature," Doctor Holliday said. "She's a native flower of Georgia, beautiful, delicate, and sweet."

That made both Mattie and Katie laugh. "I doubt you ever called Roxie delicate to her face, Mattie said.

A man in a sheepskin coat opened the doors. "Stage is comin'," he yelled before jumping back outside and into the brisk cold.

Mattie wrapped her heavy wool shawl around her shoulders and stood. "It's been over a year since I've seen her and that was when she was still in the hospital." She tucked a stray red curl behind her ear and adjusted her bonnet. "Do I look alright?"

"You are thinner, but much the same as last I saw you," Katie said as she stood to join Mattie who walked with purpose toward the doors.

Outside the big brick hotel, a driver pulled at the reins to halt his team and bring the stage to a halt on the muddy, sloping street. The shotgun rider jumped down and opened the doors while the driver began gathering bags from the top of the coach to toss down to the waiting passengers.

Mattie stood on the boardwalk and craned her neck to get a look at the people disembarking from the coach. Katie took her hand and led her down the stairs to the street level. They passed by the skittish horses and nearly got knocked over by a man trying to retrieve his luggage.

"I declare, Mattie Grace," a female voice called from behind, "you'd better watch out or you're gonna end up in this horrid mud."

Mattie turned to see a smiling Roxie with her leather cases already in hands. She ran to her petite, blonde friend and scooped her up into her arms with tears of joy, pain, and relief washing down her freckled cheeks.

"Oh, Rox, I've missed you so," Mattie sobbed. "I'm so glad you're here. I've been so alone."

Months of pent up grief over her baby's death, anger over Joshua's leaving, and lost hope came pouring out all at once until Mattie practically collapsed in the muddy street. Katie and the doctor took the sobbing, young woman in hand and helped her back into the lobby where they eased her onto an empty divan where she continued to cling to Roxie and sob.

"John, my love," Katie said to the doctor, "why don't you go to the bar and bring us a bottle of bourbon if they have it. It's what both ladies prefer to drink, if I am remembering correctly." She pushed the thin man toward the curtained entrance to the saloon area.

A few minutes later he returned carrying a silver tray with a bottle of amber liquid and four glasses. He set the tray on a side table and filled the glasses.

"Here you go ladies," he said as he passed cut crystal glasses to each woman before downing his in one gulp, followed by a long fit of coughing. He refilled his glass and drank it down quickly to ease the cough.

"I hope you are much recovered, Miss Mattie," the doctor said, offering the bottle to each of them in turn."

"I am, thank you, Doctor," Mattie said, dabbing at her eyes with her embroidered kerchief.

"Katherine," he said to Katie, "why don't you treat your friends to a meal in the dining room of this fine establishment while I attend to relieving a few of the good gentlemen in Prescott of their excess cash." He bowed and walked off toward the wide staircase.

"John is right," Katie said as she emptied the bottle into her glass, "the food is very good here. We were on our way to the dining room when we saw Mattie. Shall we dine?"

"I hope they offer more than spicy beans and corn tortillas," Roxie sighed. "I'd hoped to get a decent meal in Williams last night, but by the time the coach got there, all they had to offer was some stringy meat and cold beans." She rolled her blue eyes in disgust. "I'm sick to death of boiled beans."

Mattie smiled. "The cook here makes dumplings with the big desert quail that are delicious, Rox and they usually have blackberry cobbler, as well."

Roxie jumped to her feet with a look of longing on her pretty, pale face. "Let's find this dining room. I'm fairly starved to death."

Katie led the way, her silk skirt swishing around her legs as she walked. Mattie held onto Roxie's hand as if she feared the little blonde would disappear if she let go. A woman in a black dress and white ruffled apron seated them at a table by a sunny window and handed them menus. She brought a cut crystal pitcher filled with water to the table and the women ordered the quail and dumplings with green beans and hot buttered biscuits.

"Aside from the terrible food," Mattie asked, "how was your trip?"

"Long and dusty," Roxie sighed. "How was yours, Kate? I didn't expect to see you and Doc here. Where are your other traveling companions?"

"It was much like yours … long and dirty. Perhaps soon the railroads will reach this far west and we won't have to rely on horses and stage coaches." She took a long swallow of water. "After Wyatt filed his claim forms here, he and the family took a coach to Tucson where the women planned to purchase new wardrobes for Tombstone." She rolled her eyes. "Miss Bessie is funding this trip with the proceeds from the sale of her lovely House." She glanced at Roxie. "When James told us she'd sold it, I thought you might have been the buyer, Roxanna. It was an established House with a good clientele."

Roxie curled her lip. "It's a falling down heap with broken furniture and tattered drapes. She offered it to me, for three times it's worth, but I declined." She too picked up her glass of water. "I don't want any of Bessie's leavings and I certainly didn't want to fund the Earps after what happened to Ed."

"You blame them for Ed Masterson's death?" Katie asked with a raised eyebrow.

"If Wyatt had been doing his damned job patrolling the streets of Texas Town with Ed instead of worrying about his Faro table in the Long Branch or how much money Mattie Blaylock's cunny was bringing in, Ed wouldn't be dead," Roxie snarled. "Morgan and James are no better. They spent all their time holed up in the Long Branch doing I can only imagine what, while Ed, their boss, did the patrols they should have been doing."

"How are Bat and Jimmy taking it, Rox?" Mattie asked sadly. I bet Bat is a damned mess. He's the one who urged Ed to run for sheriff of Dodge even though he'd lost the use of his gun arm in that shooting last year. He must be taking it awfully bad."

"He is," Roxie said as the woman in her black uniform dress set a steaming plate of dumplings in front of her. "I honestly think fear of Bat's retribution is why the Earps high tailed it out of Dodge when they did." She turned to Katie. "I still don't understand why you and Doc are tagging after them. What's the hold Wyatt has over your man?"

Katie tapped pepper over her steaming plate of dumplings. "When they were down in Texas before I met Doc, Wyatt yelled out a warning that saved my John from taking a bullet in the back. He now feels indebted to the bastard and comes whenever he's called like a beaten pup." Katie shook her head and stabbed a dumpling with her fork.

"Why are you still here in Prescott if all the rest of them have already gone ahead?" Roxie asked.

"You know my Doc, Roxanna," Katie sighed. "He can't resist easy pickings and these mine owners and politicians in Prescott are very poor card players." She forked up some green beans. "We've already collected more in these few weeks than we did all of the last year in Dodge. This game tonight is supposed to be a big one with some men coming down from Calipatria and Flagstaff." She stuffed the beans into her mouth and chewed. "He says this will be his last game here and then we'll take a coach south in a day or two. Perhaps we can all dine together again before I go."

"That would be lovely, Katie," Roxie said between bites, but Mattie noticed her friend's face suddenly turn dark. "Did you get the news about Dora out here?"

"No," Katie said blandly, "did she finally admit practicing the Trade out of her room in The Dodge House?"

"She's dead," Roxie said sadly.

"What?" snapped Mattie, dropping her fork into her plate. "What happened? Did she get sick?"

Roxie shook her head and reached for her friend's hand across the table. "Shot in bed as she slept."

"By a customer?" Katie asked coolly. Katie had no fondness for Dora Hand, whom she thought hypocritical for hiding the fact that she took customers like they did, but hid behind her singing at The Lady Gay and The Alhambra.

"No, by a stupid kid from Texas who thought he was in love with her," Roxie said.

"Oh my god," Mattie gasped. "Poor sweet Dora."

"This boy was in her bedroom?" Katie persisted with her smug tone.

"No," Roxie sighed. "Dora was sleeping at Dog Kelly's while Dog was having some surgery over at Fort Dodge. She was in Dog's bed while another girl from The Lady Gay slept on his sofa." Roxie sipped her water. "This Kennedy kid from down in Texas thought he'd get rid of his competition for Dora's affections by shooting up Dog's cabin and killing him. He didn't know Dora and her friend were sleeping there or that Dog was at Fort Dodge."

"Did they hang the little bastard?" Mattie asked as she motioned for the waitress. "Miss would you bring us a bottle of bourbon from the bar?"

The woman looked at her oddly, but nodded and rushed away. Prescott might be a wild mining town, but three ladies in fine clothes asking for liquor from the saloon was an unusual request.

"The bastard's daddy," Roxie sneered, "owns half of Texas. Bat and his posse brought him back to Dodge, but he wired his rich daddy. He paid off the city law commission and they just sent the kid home to Texas."

"But Dog Kelly's the mayor and *head* of the city law commission," Mattie gasped. "How could he let that happen? Dora wrote me and told me Dog had asked her to marry him."

"Dog was against it, of course," Roxie sighed and shrugged her petite shoulders, "but the others set the price, the old man paid it, and they let the kid go."

"Did they give Dog his cut?" Katie asked with narrowed eyes.

Roxie sho9ok her golden head. "I wouldn't know, but it soured my stomach on Dodge City once and for all. I already had my bags packed when your letter came, Red. I'll never set foot in that God-forsaken town again." She used her biscuit to wipe the last of the savory gravy from her plate and popped it into her mouth. She washed it down with a long swallow of bourbon. "You ladies ready for some cobbler?"

Katie shook her head and smiled at Mattie. "I've never seen such a small woman eat so much."

"It's the first real food I've had since I departed on this damned trip." Roxie smiled and squeezed Mattie's hand.

Chapter 5

December 25, 1878

Roxie gazed toward the chamber pot, stretching and yawning upon her pillows. She'd woken to the inviting aroma of coffee boiling and bacon frying coming from the kitchen and smiled.

I'm glad Red is an early riser these days.

She pushed back the quilt and tugged her dressing gown down from the bedpost where she'd hung it the night before. The chill in the bedroom took her breath away and Roxie wanted nothing more than to snuggle back into the warm covers, but sunlight filtered through the lace curtains and she stuffed her arms into the velvet garment. Her feet landed on a braided rug next to the bed, and she slid her feet into her slippers as quickly as she could to avoid walking across the cold floor to the kitchen. She used the chamber pot and then walked to the kitchen.

"Mornin' Red," she greeted Mattie who stood over the stove spearing up slices of bacon and turning them in an iron skillet.

"Good morning, Rox and Merry Christmas."

"Oh my lord," Roxie sighed as she sat in one of the oak chairs around the table set for two with pretty dishes and linen napkins. "It *is* Christmas, isn't it?"

Mattie walked over carrying a steaming coffee pot and filled both their cups before setting it on a thick potholder to protect her polished oak tabletop. She bent and kissed the top of Roxie's blonde head. "Yes, it is. What would you like to do today?"

"I don't know. What do the good folks of Prescott do to celebrate Christmas?"

"I'm not certain," Mattie admitted. "This is my first Christmas here, but from the looks of the town, I'd say the women visit church and the men visit cribs."

Roxie chuckled. "I *did* note an over-abundance of both as we walked through town." She picked up her cup and inhaled the rich aroma of the coffee.

"That there are. Mines and miners come in and the first to follow are the trade girls, then the miners take some of them as wives and next come the churches. There are no *more* pious women than reformed whores," Mattie said with a giggle.

"You haven't become *reformed,* have you, Red?" Roxie asked with an impish grin and a raised blonde eyebrow. "Are you planning a trip to church for *us* today?"

"After my last visit to Malcolm Harper's church back in Mayfield, I swore them off for a lifetime," Mattie said, shaking her red curls as she pulled a pan of biscuits from the oven. "Joshua wanted a service for Emma Sue in the church proper, but we only had a graveside service. I couldn't bear to have her last moments out of the ground spent in one." Roxie saw her friend bat back a stray tear as the redhead poured a bowl of milk into the sizzling skillet of rue to make cream gravy to ladle over their biscuits.

"Then we should go pay our respects to the little one today," Roxie said and slipped an arm around Mattie's slender waist. "We can take that pretty wreath you've been decorating with all those little stuffed dolls. You're making that for her grave, I'm assumin'."

Mattie grinned nervously down at the shorter woman. "I had some little things made up already for her first Christmas," she stammered. "I couldn't bring myself to give them away when I cleaned out her room after …"

"I know, Sugar," Roxie cooed, resting her head against Mattie's heaving shoulder. "We'll go visit the little one after breakfast and sing her a Christmas song or two." She took a deep breath before continuing. "I don't suppose my little ones ever had any songs sung over them or any pretty things left on their plots. I just went off and left them all alone up there in Forestville all those years ago."

"Rox, your babies knew you loved them just like Emma Sue knew I loved her. Babies can sense the love from their mommas." Mattie hugged Roxie to her and then poured the gravy into a bowl to carry to the table with the plate of biscuits and bacon.

After their breakfast they dressed, bundled up against the cold, and walked to the churchyard where Mattie draped the wreath she'd made from braided grape vines and decorated with bright orange bittersweet berries, spikey green live oak leaves, and little stuffed dolls over the white stone carved with Emma Sue Kirby's name and the year of her birth and death. They sang *Silent Night* and walked back to the house hand-in-hand, weeping softly for their lost children, lost husbands, and lost happiness.

Snowflakes began to drift down upon their heads as they turned down the lane toward the neat little yellow house. Roxie took out her kerchief and blew her nose. "Mattie Kirby," Roxie announced as they neared the pretty butter yellow house and unlatched the white picket gate. "I'm gonna cook you a proper Christmas dinner. Do you have any sweet potatoes in that root cellar?"

"Yes, I do and there's a turkey or two hangin' in the smokehouse."

The women spent the rest of the late morning and early afternoon in the kitchen preparing their Christmas feast as snow fell, covering Prescott in a six-inch blanket of pure white. Around two Mattie answered a knock on the front door and returned to the kitchen with a pecan pie in her hands.

"Where did that come from?" Roxie asked, eyes wide with appreciation. "I haven't had a good praline pie in years."

"Mrs. Hammond sent it over with her son Jessie," Mattie said as she set the pie on the counter beside the bowl of dressing Roxie had scooped from the cavity of the turkey. "I feel bad now," Mattie sighed, staring at the pie. "I didn't make anything to take over there and that woman has been quite neighborly since we built here. She's got a house full of children she can barely feed, but she still thought to send me a pie for Christmas."

"Mattie, you pay that boy for the work he does, don't you?"

"Yes, but ..."

"But nothing," Roxie snapped. "You pay him and he gives the money to his momma. You're helping to support and feed her family. I know you tend to their hurts too and don't ask for nothin' in payment." She carried a plate of sliced turkey meat to the table. "If you waltzed up there now with a jar of peaches in hand it would look like you were playing catch up or something. Just send her a nice card saying thank you." She marched past the table and left the kitchen.

Mattie stared at the pie for another minute before taking the pot of coffee to the table. As she seated herself, Roxie returned, carrying a package wrapped with bright paper and tied with satin ribbons. Merry Christmas, Mattie." She laid the package in Mattie's lap. "I hope it fits. I had to guess at the measurements. I know I filled out some after my pregnancy, but could only guess at what your body had done."

Curious, Mattie untied the ribbons, setting them aside for use in her hair later. She carefully unfolded the bright foil paper to find a white box marked in gold with *Blanche's Place*. "What did you do?" Mattie asked with a wide grin.

"When was the last time you had a new store-bought dress?" Roxie asked sternly. "I know you, Red."

"I like to sew, Rox. I don't mind making my own clothes." She opened the box and her eyes went wide. Folded inside Mattie found a beautiful daffodil-yellow suit made from fine, soft wool with a bright white high-collared silk blouse trimmed in lace at the high collar and cuffs. A lovely cameo framed in red gold had been pinned at the neck.

"It's beautiful, Rox," Mattie stammered, blinking back tears. "Just beautiful." She set the box in the chair beside her and jumped up, leaving Roxie standing open-mouthed. Mattie returned with a package of her own and shoved it into Roxie's hands. "It's nothing quite so fine as yours, but I hope you like it." Mattie returned to her chair and ran a finger around the oval of the finely carved cameo. "It's not *all* store-bought and I was gonna send it to you for your birthday, but when I knew you were gonna be here for Christmas, I hurried up and finished it."

Roxie squeezed the soft package before undoing the bow and opening the red tissue paper wrapping. Her blue eyes sparkled when she lifted up the thick, white fox fur muff, but narrowed in confusion by the weight of it and slipped one hand inside, followed by the other. Her eyes went wide again and a smile spread across her face as her hands came back out holding two petite long-barreled Derringer pistols.

"This is magnificent, Red. I've never seen anything like it." She slipped the pistols back into their hiding places inside the concealing muff. "It couldn't be more perfect, Red," Roxie squealed, "I love it." She hugged the soft fur muff to her chest.

"I saw a picture of one in a periodical and thought of you straight away," Mattie said with a smile. "Josh had just brought me the white fox fur from a trading post in Flagstaff and when I saw those little pistols in the window at Riley's Mercantile, I knew it would be the perfect birthday present for you."

Roxie wrapped her arms around Mattie's neck. "Yes, they're absolutely perfect. I love them." She pulled out the pistols again to inspect them and spun the small cylinders on each one. "I've never seen long-barreled pistols this small. What size cartridges do they take?"

"There's a box in the package there."

Roxie rummaged through the paper and picked up a small, but heavy box. "So there is." She examined the box. "They won't make quite as big a hole as my other one does, but I'm sure they'll be a little more accurate." She waved one of the pistols over her head, smiling. "I can't wait to go out and practice."

"And I can't wait to try this on," Mattie said, brushing her hand over the soft yellow fabric again. "But I have no idea where I'm going to wear it."

"You wear suits to that office of yours. No rule says they all have to be drab and plain."

"Yes, my office," Mattie breathed softly. "I doubt it will be *my* office for very much longer. Jeramiah Harvey will have to replace Joshua soon. Men don't like dealing with a woman in business, especially men in the mining business.

"That's just ridiculous, Red," Roxie huffed as she pushed cartridges into the tiny cylinders of her new pistols. "I wrote to Jeramiah after I got here and told him he'd be a fool to replace you. He knows you've done all the real work in this office since Joshua took it over and you know all the accounts."

"But Rox, you know how it is with men. They don't trust a silly woman to take care of business. Our place is in the kitchen and the bedroom, not in an office."

"I'd wager that you and I know more about business and *men* than Joshua Kirby or any other fool Jeramiah might find to run this office," Roxie said with a mischievous smile. "We ran businesses and our business *was* men in the bedroom."

"Does Jeramiah know that?" Mattie asked, her eyes wide and aghast.

"He's known it about me for a long time and I suspect about you, as well."

"Oh my," Mattie sighed and took a sip of her coffee.

"Are you ashamed of what we did, Red, or just to have Jeramiah Harvey know it about ya?" Roxie asked as she scooped mashed sweet potatoes onto her plate.

"I'm not ashamed, Rox. We did what we had to get by. I married Joshua and warmed his bed, but he walked out just like any other customer might have when he was finished with me." She speared a piece of turkey from the china platter and put it on her plate. "Married or single, I was still just a whore, spreading my legs to keep a roof over my head." She ladled on some gravy, took a bite of the turkey, and chewed.

"Katie's got the right of it when she says men are all just pigs," Roxie said with a giggle. "Have you heard from her? Why do you think they lit out of town in the night like they did? I thought they planned to stay a few more days."

"I think it had something to do with that poker game Doc was in that night. I heard he took those fellas for somewhere near to forty thousand dollars." She sipped her coffee and rolled her eyes. "I don't imagine it was a completely honest game and they wanted to get into the loving embraces of the Earp brothers before somebody up here figured out that they'd been had."

Roxie whistled, "Forty thousand? Where'd you hear that?" She forked up some green beans.

Mattie shook her head and sighed. "I ran into Virgil Earp in town a few days ago and he told me those men from the game swore out a complaint against the doctor and wanted the marshal to go after him. Of course, the marshal had no idea where they might have gone and filed it away. I surely hope Katie knows what she's getting' into with that man."

"Katie's not stupid," Roxie sighed. "She sees him for what he is, but she loves him in her own way."

"Does she know he's dyin?"

"It's the consumption. He's had it for a long time and yes, she knows." Roxie nodded and opened her silver flask and poured some Tennessee whiskey into her coffee. "She told me back in Dodge that he'd contracted it during the War and had moved west to take advantage of the dryer climate."

"I guess she's smarter than either of *us* then," Mattie sighed and bit into a biscuit.

Roxie raised an eyebrow. "How do you figure?"

"If she had to find a man who was going to leave her anyway, at least it was gonna be for the grave and not another woman or," she reached for Roxie's flask, tipped it up and took a long swallow of the strong liquor, "some other damned foolishness."

Chapter 6

February 12, 1879

Mattie sat in the porch swing enjoying the sunny near-spring afternoon. She couldn't believe it could be so warm in February. In every other place she'd ever lived February was still winter and cold. It had actually been warm enough that day to do laundry outside and hang it out on the line. Her and Roxie's petticoats now hung, flapping in a light breeze and would soon be dry enough to take down and fold.

She glanced up at the row of fruit trees along the fence and thought they looked to be budding up already. Joshua had planted the peach, apple, and cherry trees last year before he'd even dug the foundation for the house. He'd told her the trees would grow with their family and feed them for years to come. She blinked away a tear at the thought of Joshua, their lost future together, and the family that would never come to be in their snug little house.

Roxie came strolling up to the swing dressed in the conservative dress she'd worn to the office. She joined Mattie on the swing.

"I see you've been busy today, Red. Can you fathom this unbelievable weather? Do you think spring always comes this early out here?"

"I think so. I'm gonna go up and talk to Mrs. Hammond and ask her about it and when she starts putting out her garden." Mattie wiped at her eyes and pointed to the fruit trees. "Does it look to you like the peaches are budding out already?"

Roxie stood and walked to the trees, the branches jutting up a good six inches over the blonde woman's head. "It surely does and the cherries and apples too." She studied the fat buds on the tips of the red branches. "If that's the case, you're gonna have fruit *before* fall. I never heard the like."

"I expected the cherries to fruit early, but I never expected the peaches and apples."

"I guess that's why they call the west the land of plenty. You get a long growing season out here."

"You haven't been here in July and August yet," Mattie said with a dry chuckle. "Everything dries up in the heat and the wells drop down below the bucket line. I near to died in the heat here last summer and they say it's worse down in Phoenix and Tucson."

"Why ever would people want to live there? Is it that bad in Tombstone where the mines are?"

Mattie shrugged her shoulders. "I've not been down there yet, but I have to make a trip to Tucson in the next few weeks to meet with a supplier. You think you're gonna be up for a trip on a stage so soon after taking that long trip from Dodge?"

Roxie wrinkled her nose and raised an eyebrow. "I suppose so, if I must."

"Nonsense, you don't have to go. I planned on making the trip alone before you got here. There's no reason I can't do it now."

"And be stuck here alone to tend the office? Not on your life, Red. If you're travelin' to the big city, I'm goin' with ya. I'm your assistant, aren't I?"

"Yes, you are and in the morning I'm sending a telegram to Jeramiah to make it official."

"Do you think he'll be alright with putting me on the payroll as an official Harvey and Edwards's employee?"

"I don't see why not, but are *you* alright with a ten dollar a month salary?" Mattie smiled sheepishly at her friend. "We used to make ten dollars in a few hours in the cribs."

"Yes, but I will only have to get dressed once and stay dressed all day," Roxie said with a broad smile and a wink.

***

After coffee and a breakfast of biscuits with butter and jam the women walked together the three blocks into town. Mattie handed her the key and left Roxie to open the office while she stopped at the telegraph office along the wide boardwalk just down the street.

"Good morning Mrs. Kirby," Mr. Grady greeted her as she walked in. "What can I do for you today?"

"I need to send a wire to Jeramiah Harvey in Colorado Springs, Mr. Grady."

"Do you want to dictate it or do you have it written out already, ma'am?"

Mattie reached into her bag and drew out a folded piece of paper with her note to Jeramiah printed on it. "Here you go." She handed him the paper and stood by while he read it over.

"Mr. Kirby isn't coming back then?" He asked, narrowing his eyes.

"No," Mattie said reluctantly, "Mr. Kirby will be continuing on at the mines in Colorado."

"My brother Miles has mine experience," he said excitedly. "Should I have him write to this Mr. Harvey about assuming Mr. Kirby's position as the company's purchasing agent here in Prescott?"

"Mr. Grady, I'm sure your brother is a fine man," Mattie said cautiously. "But I don't know that Mr. Harvey has any intention of making any changes here."

"You mean he's thinking on keeping *you,* a woman, on here in the position?" Grady said incredulous. "You can't possibly expect mine managers or suppliers to take a woman seriously as a purchasing agent for a major mining concern?"

"I haven't had any problems thus far dealing with them."

"But the job was your husband's and not *yours*. All those wires you sent were signed as coming from Mr. Kirby and not from you. They thought they were dealing with an actual man in the position and not his *female* office assistant," Grady sneered. "My brother has a family to support and is a good, God-fearing man. He deserves to have the job if it's available."

Men like Grady made Mattie want to scream and pull her hair out. He sat in this little office sending notes all day and she suspected the skinny little bastard had never done a day of real work in his life.

"Do whatever you'd like, Mr. Grady, but as far as I know Mr. Harvey hasn't had any complaints about my performance in the office here."

"Women like you are what are going wrong with this country, Mrs. Kirby," Grady snarled. "You can say whatever you like about Mr. Kirby's leaving, but I think I know the right of it. He left you because he's a decent and honorable man and saw you for the uppity, loose woman you really are, trying to take jobs away from honest *men* who need them to support their families. You should get down on your knees and beg God's forgiveness for your self-righteousness, Mrs. Kirby."

Mattie opened her mouth to reply, but closed it for fear of what would come spewing out. "Put that telegram on the company account, please," she said, turned, and opened the door to make her exit.

"I'll ask the church to pray for you, Mrs. Kirby," he said and began tapping out a telegram. She seriously doubted it to be the one she'd given him to send.

Mattie slammed the door behind her and stormed down the mud-caked boardwalk to the office of Harvey an Edwards Mining Enterprise. She slammed the door there too before stomping across the wooden planks to her desk and dropping into her chair.

"What the hell bee's got under your bonnet, Red?" Roxie snapped her head up and asked wide-eyed.

"Don't send anymore wires from Grady's office here. I seriously doubt they'll be sent." Mattie related her conversation with Grady to her friend.

"The son-of-a-bitch really said he was gonna ask the damned church to pray for ya?" Roxie asked with a smirk.

"Like I should have turned and said thank you for his care of my sinful soul."

"If he only knew," Roxie sputtered, laughing. "To hell with the son-of-a-bitch, Red, I'm gonna post another letter to Jeramiah. If he has a mind to replace you, I'll go to Colorado Springs and give him a piece of my mind in person." She smiled broadly. "I'll take my new muff and show off my new little pistols. You should write him too."

"You're a dear friend, Rox, but this is something I've been expecting since Joshua left. I can't expect Jeramiah to keep me on here without Joshua. Grady was right. The job was Joshua's and not mine. I just helped him out."

"Because he could hardly read or add two columns of numbers together," Roxie sputtered. "Will only offered him the job because he knew you'd be going along to do the actual office work. Josh is big and a formidable man, but he couldn't carry off this job without you. Jeramiah Harvey knows that."

"I hope you're right, Rox. I don't know what I'll do without this job. It took all my savings to buy the land, build the house here, and furnish it. I only have a little over a hundred dollars left in the bank."

"Can you sell the house?" Roxie asked hesitantly.

"I don't know. You know how things are. The land and house are Joshua's legally. They're deeded in his name."

"I have money." Roxie said, wringing her hands upon her desk. "I can get you a lawyer. Joshua Kirby abandoned you without support and we can get proof the money to buy the land and build the house came from your account at the bank in Dodge." Roxie winked at her friend from across the room. "We're old hands at gathering evidence and proving claims. Now, aren't we?" She said, referring to their sojourn from Dodge to Colorado Springs to prove Willard Edward's claim to part ownership in the Domingo Gold Mine and Will's subsequent windfall from that mine's back earnings.

"I suppose we are," Mattie sighed, "but I don't know that I have the strength to fight in me anymore, Rox."

"Red, you're one of the strongest women I've ever known." Roxie walked over and took Mattie's cold, trembling hands. "I'm gonna sit here and write another letter to Jeramiah then we'll walk ourselves up town and find a lawyer. This town is full of politicians and lawyers. I'm sure we can find one who can get your house put into your name and get you divorced from that big dumb ox you married. How much do you think your house is worth?"

"I couldn't say for certain," Mattie said and shrugged her shoulders, "but with all the folks movin' in up here with the mining and such, I'd say it's worth a good eight hundred or a thousand. It's only on an acre of ground, but it has garden space, the fruit trees, and the barn."

"That's really good. Back in Dodge the same house wouldn't sell for more than two hundred dollars on a good day."

"Yes, but Dodge is just a cow town. People want ranches and farms there, not little houses in town."

"I suppose you're right," Roxie sighed. "I'm glad I didn't buy one when I went back there and just took a room in The Dodge House." Roxie smiled at her friend. "Maybe *I'll* buy your house and *you* can move into the little bedroom."

"The way the town is growing," Mattie laughed, "it would be a good investment and it *is* the Territorial Capital."

Chapter 7

March 9, 1879

Roxie sat uncomfortably on the rocking stage headed south from Prescott toward Phoenix and then on to Tucson with Mattie sitting beside her. The other passengers on the coach were a stout woman of middle years and her two children, a boy of about eight and a girl of possibly ten or eleven. The girl wore a ridiculously big bow in her limp dishwater-blonde hair and the boy's nose ran with him continually wiped it with the sleeve of his plaid flannel shirt.

The trip would take two days' hard travel to reach Phoenix and another two to reach Tucson, where Mattie had arranged to meet a tool supplier from California. The night before had been spent at a stage stop outside the mining town of Crown King where they'd eaten beans in a cantina and slept in uncomfortable narrow cots, reminding Roxie of her trip west from Dodge. With luck, the driver had told them that morning, they would reach Phoenix by night fall and stay in a nice hotel near the downtown stage office.

The boy sneezed again. Roxie pulled out a kerchief and handed it to him. "Here, young man," she said curtly. "A respectable young gentleman does *not* use his shirt-sleeve to clean his dirty nose."

"I beg your pardon, madam," the child's mother spoke up and grabbed the embroidered kerchief away from the child to toss back at Roxie. "I don't need a woman like you tending to *my* children."

"Well," Mattie said, lifting her eyes up from her periodical, "somebody certainly should. Just exactly what sort of woman do you think my friend is?" She glared at the woman from her seat.

"Momma says you are dirty parlor women," the girl said shyly. "Momma they don't look dirty to me. They look clean and have right pretty clothes. They look just like the pretty clothes in the periodicals you sneak from the apothecary and hide from Poppa."

"Poppa knows about the periodicals, Momma," chimed in the boy who sniffed loudly and wiped his nose on his sleeve again. He turned back to address Roxie and Mattie. "My poppa owns a silver mine in Tombstone and we're gonna be rich."

"If parlor women have pretty clothes like them, Momma, then I want to be a parlor woman when I grow up," the girl said boldly and reached out to touch the soft wool of Mattie's yellow skirt.

With an appalled look on her face, her mother slapped the girl's hand away from Mattie's skirt. "Watch your mouth, Martha Jean McGuire or I'll was it out with lye soap."

"Mrs. McGuire you have a lovely family and I wish you well in Tombstone," Roxie said and bent over to stuff the kerchief into the snot-nosed boy's shirt pocket. "You be a gentleman and clean your nose on a kerchief and not your sleeve, young man. Rich young silver barons shouldn't use their shirt-sleeves like common street urchins."

The boy glanced sideways to his frowning mother, took out the kerchief, and blew his nose loudly. "Thank you kindly, ma'am," he told Roxie before returning the soiled kerchief to his pocket.

They rode quietly for the next two hours, aside from the children's bickering over this thing and that and the mother trying to shush them. Mattie leafed through her fashion periodical and Roxie tried to concentrate on a romance novel about a rich rancher's daughter in

Texas who'd fallen in love with a wild outlaw cowboy and wanted to run away with him.

The people who write this nonsense have never been to the west. That is obvious and they must think we're all daft who read this stuff. No young woman in her right mind is going to give up a good life in a clean ranch house with servants and three hot meals a day to run off with an uneducated cowpoke to live amongst the coyotes and cactus, dodging the bullets of lawmen that are after him. This is written for airheaded little girls in the cities who have no idea of what goes on in the real world.

Roxie slammed the book shut as gunfire suddenly erupted around them and the coach jerked to a halt, launching the boy they'd come to know as Peter into Roxie's lap and Martha Jean into Mattie's. Their mother quickly pulled them back to encircle them protectively in her meaty arms.

"What do you think is going on," she asked the women with her eyes wide with fright.

Roxie put her book onto the seat between her and Mattie, slipped her drawstring bag onto her wrist and slid her hands into her white fox-fur muff before the door to the coach was yanked open and a man with a red kerchief tied across the lower half of his face stuck his head inside to peer at the passengers.

"Looks like we got us a real treat today fellas. The coach is full of women and kids," he yelled to the others. Roxie heard another man yelling orders to the drivers above. "This here's a robbery, ladies," he said and took off his wide-brimmed, sweat-stained hat. "Get yourselves out here and drop your valuables into my hat for safekeeping," he ordered with a wink and a chuckle.

"Just do as he says," Roxie said to Mrs. McGuire, who looked to be about to make a fuss, "and don't say anything to get them riled." She took off her earbobs and dropped them into the hat Peter held in his trembling little hands.

The big man watched as Mattie took the cameo from her collar and dropped it into the hat. "That's good, now get out so me and the boys can have a good look at ya." He grabbed Mrs. McGuire by the chubby wrist and yanked her from the coach. She went out with a loud yelp, her two children following close behind, holding onto her skirt. Roxie saw him reach out and yank the little gold cross from Martha Jean's neck and add it to the jewelry already in his dusty hat.

Roxie and Mattie stepped out of the coach and Roxie could see the lust in the man's eyes as he looked them up and down. Mattie assisted Roxie as she had both hands tucked into her muff.

"Woo hoo, boys, we got us some quality women here today," the man yelled and brushed Roxie's cheek with his rough, dirty hand before he turned his gaze back to Mrs. McGuire and her cowering children. "And look here, Jesus, a fat one just the way you like 'em." He leered down at Martha Jean quivering in behind her mother's skirts. "Rans there's even one here the way you like 'em before their first bloody cunny." He gave an obscene chuckle.

"Sir, there's really no reason to frighten the children and their poor dear mother with your officious, foul talk," Roxie said in her sweetest southern drawl to the big man in the red kerchief.

He glared at Roxie with big dark eyes. The wind ruffled his greasy black hair. "This is a foul land, missy and if they don't know it yet, it's sure as hell time they learned."

Roxie glanced up at the shotgun rider whose hand eased toward a gun tucked close beside his boots. She shook her head slightly, hoping to stay his hand. Three men other than the three on this side of the coach stood around the strong box the driver had thrown down, attempting to open it. The shotgun rider pulling his weapon at this point would only endanger the children more than need be.

The man in the red kerchief, who seemed to be the leader of this group of ruffians, stepped to Mattie and ran his hand over her red curls and touched the tip of his big revolver to one of her ample bosoms.

I like me a red-headed woman and one with big bosoms is surely a plus." He yanked Mattie's drawstring bag from her wrist and shook it. Coins jingled inside and he dumped the bag into his hat. "And a rich one, too." He looked back into his hat and shook it. "I count three gold eagles and four silvers." He whistled and pinched Mattie's bosom, leaving dark smudges on the yellow fabric of her jacket.

"You're a beast, sir," Mrs. McGuire yelled, clutching her crying children close, "stealing from defenseless women and children. You should be ashamed."

"Rans," he called to a skinny man with a blue kerchief over his face, tending the riderless horses, "get over here and drag this hairless little cunny under the wagon so her momma can hear her squeal when you pop her open for the first time." He looked to a wide-eyed Mrs. McGuire and added, "Unless her poppa's already done that."

"You disgusting … filth," Mrs. McGuire howled.

The skinny man came trotting over and yanked Martha Jean from her mother's grasp and began dragging the screaming child toward the underside of the coach. "Thanks, Ned," he called to the man in the red kerchief, "this is gonna be fun." He pulled the bow from Martha Jean's hair and tossed it toward her wailing mother.

"You're a disgusting piece of shit," Roxie said to Ned, whose eyes smiled as he watched Rans dragging the wailing Martha Jean away from her mother.

"And just what do you have there, Blondie," Ned sneered from beneath his kerchief and reached for the bag hanging from Roxie's wrist.

"Well, if you really want to know," Roxie said and pulled her hands free of her white fur muff with a Derringer pistol cocked in each one. Her first shot took Ned squarely between the eyes and her second and third hit Rans in his butt cheeks as he bent to push Martha Jean beneath the stage.

Roxie's gunplay took the others by surprise and signaled the shotgun driver to grab his weapon and in no time at all the gang of outlaws lay moaning in the dust or dead. The horses Rans had been tending scattered with the noise and the stage's driver had to pull tightly on the reins to keep his team from bolting.

As soon as Rans released his hold on her, Martha Jean rolled from beneath the coach and ran into her mother's arms. They quickly climbed back into the coach, stepping over a moaning Rans, who lay on his belly as blood seeped from the two small bullet holes in his skinny ass cheeks.

The shotgun driver had joined them after collecting the cash from the downed men and returning it to the strong box.

"You handled yourself right fine, ma'am," he said to Roxie as he helped her back into the coach and returned their belongings from Ned's dirty hat. "We've been having trouble along this line for a while now. This bunch has held up a half dozen coaches over as many months and killed two good men. It's why they hired me on." He helped Mattie up and closed the door behind her. "I'm really sorry you ladies had to be put through that."

Rans, who still lie curled on the ground whined, "What about me? You can't leave me here to bleed to death."

Mattie leaned out the window and snarled at the man, "Oh shut up, you disgusting piece of offal. She could have aimed a bit more to the center and blown off your useless ballocks and cock."

"Would that she had," Mrs. McGuire called after her, "worthless, perverted scum. I hope the coyotes find you and chew your innards out."

"You can't leave me here like this," the man howled as the driver climbed back atop the coach.

"Just get your sorry ass up and collect one of your horses," the driver said as he urged the team on its away.

The women and children settled in as the coach began to roll southward once again. Roxie picked up her book and opened it to the page she'd been reading, but couldn't find any interest in it.

"I can't believe that driver said the line knew about the danger of a holdup, but still sold tickets without warning us," Mrs. McGuire said sourly. "I've a mind to write the governor when I get to Tombstone and lodge a complaint."

"Don't bother," Roxie said over her book, "the stage lines pay off the state officials to keep that sort of thing off their backs."

"You're better off to go directly to the newspapers," Mattie said. "Tell them every horrible detail to embarrass the stage line and maybe cost them future passengers. That's the best way to get even with the company."

"I think she's right, Momma," Martha Jean said to her mother. "We'll tell our story to the newspaper and everybody will know what those terrible men did to us. Then people will know and be ready if men attack them on the stage, too."

Mrs. McGuire took her daughter's hand. "We'll talk about it later Martha Jean. I just want to get to Tombstone and your father where we'll be safe."

"I'd feel safe if I knew how to shoot guns like Miss Roxie," Martha Jean said and gave Roxie a coy smile. "If all parlor women can shoot guns, I *know* I want to be a parlor woman when I grow up."

"When y'all get to Tombstone, Martha Jean, ask your poppa to teach you to shoot," Roxie said staring at Mrs. McGuire. "Unfortunately there are more men like those back there than good men like your poppa in this territory and every woman should be able to protect herself, her family," she took Mattie's hand, "and her friends when needs be."

Chapter 8

March 12, 1879

Mattie sat with Roxie in the dining room of the El Cortez Hotel in Tucson, sipping iced lemon water as they waited for the man from Bailey Steel out of Colton, California, where she ordered mining tools for Harvey and Edwards' Tombstone and Globe mining concerns. She'd made this appointment months ago and it irked her that the man was late.

"I think we've been stood up, Red," Roxie said with a sheepish grin. She took a sip of the sour drink and furrowed her brow. "This stuff is refreshin', but I'd be happier if we could sweeten it with a splash from my flask." She sat her bag on the table and went to reach inside for her silver flask."

"No, Rox, this is a business meeting and we have to be clearheaded. These salesmen are a shifty lot and will try to slip things by on ya if you're not careful. No liquor until the meeting is over," she said and glanced around the opulent dining room as the big clock in the lobby chimed half past eleven, "if he ever shows up."

A handsome young gentleman in a crisp blue suit came walking up to their table. "Mrs. Kirby and Mrs. Edwards? He extended his hand. "I'd recognize you anywhere Mrs. Edwards, but the artist's rendering in the newspaper didn't do you justice. You're much more beautiful in person."

After they'd reached Phoenix and reported the incident on the trail, the women had been interviewed by reporters from the newspaper.

One had been an Associated Press reporter and had assured them the story would soon be going nationwide with an artist's rendering of the event on the front pages of every paper in an AP affiliated city.

True to his word, the following g day's paper had featured their story with a drawing of Roxie pointing her little pistols in defense of little Martha Jean's virtue and the rest of their lives against a lurking group of masked bandits. The stage drivers cowered in the seats above the fray, looking frightened. Mattie didn't think that had been fair to the poor drivers, but did justice to the stage line whose name was featured boldly on the rendering of the coach in the drawing.

"Why thank you ever so much, sir," Roxie said, taking his outstretched hand, "but might we know who we have the honor of addressin'?"

"But of course, forgive me. I'm Marvin Howard with Bailey Steel and I believe we have an appointment." He turned from Roxie to Mattie. "I'm sorry to keep you waiting. My coach from Benson was late getting in. I only just arrived in town and had to get from my hotel to this one."

"It's perfectly understandable, Mr. Howard," Mattie said. "Please have a seat."

The waiter came by and Mr. Howard ordered a coffee and a glass of iced water. He reached into his leather satchel and produced a crisp sheet of paper which he handed to Mattie. "I just came from a meeting with your man Adams in Tombstone and read the account of your harrowing experience as I traveled. This is the order that he's requested to get by for the next quarter of production. I just need your signature at the bottom as purchasing agent for Harvey and Edwards to get the gears turning." He smiled at Roxie who ignored him and sipped her cold lemon water.

"These numbers seem to be a bit higher than the ones he sent to me last month before I arranged this meeting," Mattie said, studying Howard's list. "I'll have to go back to my office and look over Mr. Adams' last correspondence and then confer with Mr. Harvey in Colorado Springs before I can give you an order, Mr. Howard." She slid the sheet of paper into her own satchel and then smiled at the frowning salesman.

"I can't guarantee those prices for more than ten days, Mrs. Kirby. With the expanding railroads buying up every ounce of steel produced, the prices are very volatile, but I don't suspect you'd understand such things."

"I'm more than aware of the effect of supply and demand on the prices of goods and services, Mr. Howard," Mattie said with an annoyed frown, "but this is a rather large order and I have to discuss it with Mr. Harvey in Colorado Springs before signing off on it. The money is his, after all. I should be back in the office a week from today and will look over my notes and wire Mr. Harvey. I'm certain I'll have his reply well before your ten days."

"I suppose that's the difference between dealing with a man and dealing with a woman in circumstances such as these," he sighed. "A man can make a decision without asking for permission first while a weak woman never will."

Mattie looked over at the man and smiled, though she really wanted nothing more than to throttle him where he sat. "While Harvey and Edwards has regularly done business with Bailey Steel Fabricators, I've recently been contacted by Bethlehem in Ohio and their prices are very competitive. I have to give them some serious consideration, Mr. Howard. That's only sound business practice; man or woman."

"But the shipping costs from Ohio would surely push your cost up beyond consideration, Mrs. Kirby," he said confidently.

"They've promised me the prices are quoted as shipped from their local distributors and those would be quite competitive with Bailey." Mattie picked up her satchel and stood. "I'll contact you with my and Mr. Harvey's decision in the matter, Mr. Howard," Mattie said and walked away without waiting for him to offer his hand.

"If I were you, Mr. Howard," Roxie said sweetly as she stepped past the stunned salesman, "I'd study hard on how to extract my big foot from my mouth and how I'm gonna explain to my bosses back at Bailey how I just lost their company one of the largest mining accounts in the Arizona and more than likely Colorado Territories."

She hurried up to catch her friend. "Hold on, Red. It wasn't me who was the big ass back there."

"I know, Rox, I'm sorry." She stopped and looked at the clock in the lobby. "Our stage doesn't leave for another hour. Let's have a drink."

"I thought you'd never ask," Roxie sighed and turned toward the saloon entrance.

They walked into a quiet room with only one girl in a frilly dress leaning against the polished bar and a barman standing behind the counter. They took seats at a green felt-topped table and waited for the bored looking girl to come and take their order.

"I think you fine *senoras* are in the wrong place," the pretty dusky-skinned girl with long black hair said with a bit of a sneer, "this is the saloon not the salon."

"We're quite aware of where we are," Roxie snapped in the same crude tone. "Bring us a bottle of your best whiskey and two glasses."

"Yes, *senora*," the girl said and walked away.

"Am I mistaken or did that little tart just talk to us like we were two used up old women?" Roxie asked with a frown.

"Look at us Rox, dressed in our conservative clothes with our hair done up in buns on the tops of our heads. I'm almost thirty and you're pushin' thirty-five. She can't be more than eighteen. To her, we *are* used up old women." Mattie laughed while Roxie sat frowning after the girl.

"Oh, my lord," Roxie sighed, "you're right. Where'd the years go, Red? It seems it was just last year we were on *The Ruby Queen* talkin' about our plans to have grand adventures out here in the west."

Mattie patted her friend's hand. "And we've certainly had them, Rox. We've had more adventures than any poor farm girl from Mayfield, Kentucky, ever dreamed of havin'. I spent time playing piano on a Mississippi riverboat, met gamblers and gunslingers, traveled first-class in fancy rail cars, ate and slept in some of the grandest hotels, and did it all with the finest friend a woman could ever have hoped to have."

The young woman brought their bottle and filled their glasses. "May I ask what two fine ladies like you are doing ordering whiskey in the saloon at the El Cortez?" she asked.

"Grab yourself a glass, young lady and join us," Roxie offered.

The girl left and returned with a glass which she filled after she sat. "My name is Rosalinda," she said and swallowed the glass of whiskey.

"How old are you, Rosalinda?" Mattie asked.

"*Dies y siete* … seventeen," she replied. "*Mi papa* he run this saloon."

"And he lets you drink this swill?" Roxie asked, taking the shot glass from the girl's hand. "You should still be playing with dolls, not serving drinks in a saloon dressed like a trollop."

"I don't know this word trollop, but *mi mama* made this dress for me to make good tips from the men who come in here. I have six younger *hermanos y hermanas.* I must help to support them with the money I earn here." She looked back toward the bar where the older barman stood watching.

"That your *papa* over there?" Roxie asked.

"No, *mi tio* ... my uncle. He works here too and helps to look after me," she said and smiled at the man behind the bar. He smiled back before he resumed stacking glasses.

"I'm going to give you some advice, Rosalinda and if you never listen to any advice again in your life, listen to this," Roxie said seriously. "Take part of that money you're making and hide it away for yourself. Never give it to a man for any reason. Your money is yours and no man is entitled to it, not your *papa,* your *tio,* your boyfriend, *or* your husband. Give yourself to no man. If he wants you bad enough, make him pay for it and make the price a high one. If he wants you bad enough, he'll meet your price." She took the girl's hand. "And whatever you do never trust one farther than you could pick him up and toss him. Men are liars and cheats when it comes to women. It's their nature. They can't help it, but don't let one of them take you in with sweet words. They're all lies." Roxie released the girl's hand and patted it lovingly. "Save your money and use a man for your pleasure when you will. You'll be the happier for it."

Rosalinda stared at Roxie with a serious face. "You sound like my mother and my aunt. They tell me the same things about my money and men. If you two *gringas* are saying the same, then perhaps it is true."

"They sound like smart women Rosalinda. You should listen to what they have to say," Mattie said, smiling at the pretty girl.

Her uncle yelled for her and Rosalinda rolled her eyes, but rose and went to attend to the men in fashionable suits who'd taken a seat at a table across the room.

Roxie took her flask from her bag and filled it from the bottle on the table. "This is swill, but it's all there is and I know I'm gonna need a drink or two before we get home."

"I'm sure we will," Mattie said and took another swallow. "This certainly isn't the best I've ever tasted, but it does have a kick to it."

Roxie finished refilling her flask and returned it to her bag. "I thought you had Adams' order with you in that satchel."

"I do," Mattie admitted. "I just wanted to see what that arrogant son-of-a-bitch had to say."

"He did seem a mite sure of himself. Do you think he inflated that order or Adams?" Roxie asked and took a sip of her whiskey.

"Both of them, I don't doubt. I'm sure Adams' original order is the one that would be filled and after the funds were received by Howard for the inflated one, Adams would get a split."

"Are you going to bring that to Jeramiah's attention?"

"I'll wire Adams first and see what he has to say. I don't want to get him into trouble if he really needs the extra equipment." Mattie used her sleeve to wipe perspiration from her brow. "But I won't countenance a swindler trying to use me either."

The clock in the lobby chimed. "We'd better check to make certain our things are in the lobby," Mattie said and stood. "The stage back to Phoenix should be here soon."

"Just what my ass needs," groaned Roxie, "another week in a bouncing coach. I hope we have this one to ourselves. I can do without the whining brats and their mouthy mommas."

Chapter 9

April 8, 1879

Warm late winter had turned into warmer early spring and the fruit trees on Mattie's little property had indeed burst into full bloom by the time they'd returned from Tucson. Roxie, who'd taken the day off from the office to attend to some chores around the house, stood tying strips of torn cloth onto the spindly branches to flutter in the breezes and protect the tiny new fruits from greedy birds when she looked up to see a rider coming up the lane toward the house.

Oh, dear Jesus, it can't be. What's that son-of-a-bitch doing here?

Roxie loosened the knot securing her wide-brimmed straw sun hat and let it fall to the back of her head as she walked to meet the big man riding up to the house. She met him at the gate of the picket fence before he could dismount.

"What the hell are you doing here, Joshua Kirby?" Roxie demanded in a sour tone as she stood to bar his way to the gate. "Red's still at the office, but she should be here within the hour."

"Hello, Miss Roxie," Mattie's estranged husband said as he jumped down from his big, black mare.

The poor beast probably needs a rest after lugging that giant around on her poor back.

"Why don't you lead that poor animal to the trough while you wait for her?"

Joshua nodded to the petite woman and tied the panting animal to the post by the water trough at the end of the lane just inside the fence around the small barnyard. Mattie's buggy horse trotted over to the big man with an expectant winnie. Joshua patted the animal's neck and then reached into his jacket pocket and took out a cube of sugar that he offered to the beast.

"That's a good girl, Daisy. Have you missed Claudette and me?"

"You've been missed," Roxie said as she watched him attend to the animals. "Now what in hell's name are you doin' here, Joshua? Don't you think you've caused enough misery, blamin' Red for her baby's death and just walkin' out on her?" Roxie drew her hand back and would have slapped the man had he been closer.

"I come to talk to Mattie," Joshua said as he pulled the bit from his horse's mouth. Roxie continued to frown as she watched him unbuckling the straps on his saddle.

Looks like the bastard's plannin' to stay for a while.

Joshua tugged the saddle and blanket from his mount and carried them to the barn. Roxie stood her ground at the gate as Joshua walked up.

"You gonna make me stand out here in the mud until Mattie gets here?"

"I don't know as she'd be happy with me lettin' you into *her* house."

Joshua raised a bushy eyebrow and frowned. "Sounds as she's poisoned you on me some, Miss Roxie." He turned and leaned his backside against the pine post holding up the hinged side of the gate.

"She hasn't said one damned word against you, Joshua," Roxie hissed. "You walkin' out on her the day you buried her baby poisoned me on you. Just what do you have to say for yourself on that account? How could you do such a thing and even blame her for what happened." Roxie stood with her hands on her narrow hips. "You're a son-of-a-bitch, Joshua Kirby. That sort of behavior I've come to expect from *my* husband, but I always thought you were a better man."

The big bear of a man stood cowering before the little spit-fire scowling across the fence at him. "I'm powerful sorry to have disappointed you, Miss Roxie. You know I've always held your opinion in high regard, but losing that sweet child was simply more than I could bear." He took a deep breath and brushed a tear from his broad, sunburned cheek. "I don't think I've ever loved anything more than that beautiful little bundle and when I had to stand there watchin' her strugglin' for breath in that doctor's office," he said and took off his hat to wipe his forehead with his sleeve. "Well, I lost my mind some with the fear and then the grief. I just couldn't stay in that house or look at Mattie Grace for one more minute."

"And you think *she* could? Do you think it was easy for *her* to be in this house and sit here in the lonesome quiet of it without you or her child?" Roxie shook her head in disgust. "Katie's right. All y'all men are heartless swine."

Roxie glared up at Joshua, but the pain in his big, brown eyes touched her heart. "You're a pig, Joshua Kirby, but I don't suppose I can leave you out here in the mud until Mattie gets home." She unlatched the gate and pushed it open. "Come on in. I've got to mix up the cornbread for supper, anyhow, and get it into the oven."

"Thank you, Miss Roxie." He stepped gingerly through the gate and past the little blonde woman. "What you cookin' to go with that cornbread?" He asked with a longing look in his big, brown eyes.

"Elk meat stew made with the last of the shriveled potatoes and carrots in the root cellar from last year's garden," Roxie said as she opened the back door. "And take off those muddy boots. I spent the mornin' scrubbin' this floor and I don't want you trackin' it all up before Red gets home."

Joshua took Roxie by the arm and stopped her. "I want to talk to Mattie …" he stammered. "I want to tell her I'm sorry and ask her to …" He glanced at Roxie nervously and licked his lips before continuing, "… to be my wife again."

Roxie rolled her eyes. "Don't be a fool, Joshua. You walked out on her at the worst moment in her life and made her feel like dirt." Roxie opened the screened door. "All you can do is ask, but if it was me, I'd scratch your damned fool eyes out of your head." She let out a deep breath and glared at Joshua. "Take off your damned boots."

"Yes, ma'am," he said and propped his tall frame against the house while he pulled off his dusty boots to leave on the porch. "I've surely missed your fine cookin' Miss Roxie." He inhaled deeply and smiled down at Roxie. "It smells fearsome good in here."

"Doesn't Will's Indian wife cook for you?" Roxie asked with an irritated glance at the big man who'd taken a seat at the table without so much as a by your leave.

Typical man! He walks off and leaves the place, but comes back and acts like it's his right to be here like he'd never gone in the first place.

"Miss Alia don't live with Bump no more," Joshua said nervously. "She got wind of her people up in the mountains and lit out to find 'em about a month after I joined back up with him. Me, Will, and the boy have been doin' for ourselves," he said with a sheepish grin, "and you know how Bump is in the kitchen."

"He still burnin' the bacon?" Roxie asked as she scooped cornmeal into a bowl. She had to smile, hearing Joshua refer to Willard as Bump—the old nickname Joshua had given to him because of the head injury he'd received when Will had been attacked all those years ago on a mountain trail by Marty Rowe.

"That and everything else," Joshua grunted. "The boy's a fair cook and tries to beat Bump into the kitchen most days."

"But Jumping Elk can't be more than six or seven," Roxie said aghast. "You two are making a seven-year-old child do the cooking for all of you?"

"The boy likes to eat," Joshua said with a grin and shrugged his broad shoulders. "He knows that if he wants to eat food that's not burned to a crisp; he has to cook it."

Roxie shook her head as she cracked eggs and then mixed them vigorously into her batter. "You should be ashamed. Why don't you just hire a woman to do the cookin' and cleanin'. Are y'all makin' the poor child do your laundry too?"

"No," Joshua said, "Bump takes the laundry to a washerwoman in town, but he don't think we should spend the money for a full time cook and housekeeper, too."

"It's not like he can't afford one," Roxie huffed. "Will is a rich man. I'm surprised he doesn't have a whole passel of women lined up at the door just beggin' to take care of his cookin' and cleanin' in the hopes he might make it a permanent position with a weddin' ring."

"He probably would if ..." he said hesitantly, "if it weren't for the boy and that he'd taken Miss Alia to wife. None of the women or girls want to take up with an Indian-lover and don't want to be called momma by no half-breed pup."

"That's just ridiculous," Roxie said sadly, "Jumping Elk is a sweet child."

"That he is," Joshua said as he took the cup of coffee Roxie handed to him. "You should have seen the way the poor thing cried and carried on when Miss Alia told them she was leaving them and not comin' back. It damn near broke my heart."

"Why isn't she coming back?" Roxie asked as she slid the pan of cornbread batter into the oven.

"It was hard on her in the mining camps," Joshua said. "The women wouldn't have nothing to do with her and the men ... well the men were ..."

"Men," Roxie snapped, suddenly feeling pity for the young Indian woman who'd stolen her husband away from her.

I don't even know for certain that Alia did any stealing. Maybe Willard Edwards simply couldn't keep his cock in his pants while I was locked away in that hospital. The only thing that girl had ever known was servitude to men. She'd been a slave in the Shoshone camp when me and Will rescued her and nothing more than a whore passed around to her Shoshone master's friends. Maybe Alia thought it was her place to warm Will's bed in my absence. I know for certain she cared for Jumping Elk very much.

"Didn't Will treat her well?" Roxie asked without being snide.

Joshua shrugged his broad shoulders. "I guess he treated her alright. I know he didn't care for her near as much as he cared about you, Miss Roxie." He took a long drink from the dainty china cup, emptying it in one swallow.

"When he come upon that newspaper with the picture of you on the front page, he read it to me over and over again. Then he cut out that picture of you shootin' up them bastards and put it in his fiddle case with his other important papers."

"Well, doesn't that make me just feel special," Roxie said with a scowl on her face. "He put me into his precious fiddle case."

"You shouldn't feel that way, Miss Roxie. You was real sick in that hospital and that old doctor said you might be like you was just layin' there starin' off at nothin' for a long time to come. He had to have someone to attend to the boy and …"

"And attend to him," Roxie snorted. "I understand exactly how it was, Joshua. I was in a hospital bed and not *his* bed. Did you know that when he took off with Alia and the boy he'd only paid for my hospital stay in that fancy sanatorium until the end of the month? If I hadn't come out of it when I did, I'd have been sent to the state asylum to lie on a pallet on the floor in my own piss and shit. Didn't he tell you that?"

Joshua glanced nervously around the room. "No, he never told me that. He just told me that Jeramiah was pressin' him to get back to the mines and that you wanted a divorce anyhow. The boy needed a mother, so he did what he thought would make everyone happy."

"Willard Edwards did what Willard Edwards thought would make *him* happy," she snapped and peeked into the oven to check on her cornbread. "He wanted a wife and a mother for his child and I know he was never really happy with me. He didn't want a whore for a wife and after I lost the baby, Alia was the better choice. She could have given him more children and fit the family better with Jumping Elk. People would accept the boy if he had an Indian wife, rather than a white one. I understand that," Roxie sighed.

"You understand what?" Mattie said as she stepped quietly through the door and into the warm kitchen. She gave Joshua a withering glance. "Hello, Joshua. Did I miss the wire telling me you were coming for a visit?"

Joshua stood and stared nervously at his estranged wife. "I'm … I'm sorry Mattie. Me and Will seen that newspaper story about that stage robbery and we was both worried about you and Miss Roxie here." He grinned weakly at Roxie, avoiding Mattie's glare. "We was between assignments, so I thought I'd come down and check up on you and have a quiet talk."

"Wasn't that sweet of him Red?" Roxie brought a stack of plates to the table along with forks and placed them in their respective spots around the oak table. "We have Elk stew and I invited Joshua to join us," she said, rolling her eyes. "He was just tellin' me that Alia left them to go back to her people in the mountains and that they've had Will's little boy doin' the cookin' for 'em. Can you imagine that; two grown men dependin' on a seven-year-old boy to do their cookin' for 'em?" She went back to the stove and pulled out the muffin pan with six yellow corn muffins standing high. Roxie set them aside and lifted the steaming pot of stew off the stove to carry to the table.

Roxie returned to the stove to retrieve the muffins while Mattie took a seat at the table, trying to avoid her husband's uneasy glances. "Will probably still burns everything he touches. It makes sense, I suppose," she said and glanced nervously at Roxie. "You'd never let him in *your* kitchen over much as I recall."

"He's a danger to good food when fire's involved," Joshua agreed with a chuckle. "That's for certain and the boy's a right good cook, too." He smiled up at Roxie. "Not near as fine as you, Miss Roxie, but a lot better than Bump or me."

"I can just imagine," Roxie said, winking at Mattie. "I can just imagine."

They ate their dinner, chatting about the mines in Colorado and gossip throughout the Harvey and Edwards's system. After Joshua had scraped his third plate of stew clean with the last cornbread muffin, he looked over at Roxie and said, "Miss Roxie would you mind giving Mattie and me the kitchen? We need to do us some talkin' private like."

"Joshua," Mattie snapped. "Roxie lives here now and you can't just come waltzing in here ordering her around."

"It's alright, Red," Roxie said and stood. "You two can do the dishes while I go out and take the wash off the line." She left Mattie and Joshua sitting uncomfortably together at the table.

Mattie stood and began picking up the china plates to stack in the sink. She pumped water over them before putting the empty stew pot under the spout to fill and set upon the stove to heat for wash water.

"What's so all-fired important, Joshua that you had to ride all the way down here from Colorado to say?"

The big man stood and joined Mattie at the sink with the delicate empty coffee cups in his brawny hands. "I thought we should talk about what's to become of us, Mattie. I've been thinkin' hard on it and I'm sorry for leavin' like I done." Joshua took a deep breath and put his arms around Mattie's slender waist. "You look right good, woman," he said and began nuzzling at her ear. His hands creeped up to her bosoms.

"What the hell do you think you're doing," the redhead snapped angrily and pulled away. "Did you think I was just gonna melt into your arms in gratitude for saying you're sorry for being a goddamned ass or something?"

"I said I was *sorry,* Mattie," he said, staring down into her angry green eyes. "What more do you want from a man? I'm your husband and you belong with me."

Anger flared in Mattie's eyes with that comment. "I *belong* to you?" She seethed. "Are you planning to stay here in Prescott with me and resume your place at the office?"

He shook his head. "No, I'm not cut out for work in no silly office. You know that better than anybody. I need to be out in the wilds. I like livin' in the minin' camps." He smiled broadly. "You'll like it too, Mattie. I done made all the arrangements for us."

"What?" she gasped, wide-eyed. "I'm not going anywhere. My home is here and my baby is buried here. My job is here. I'm not going anywhere."

Joshua stared at her with confusion on his face. "But I thought you'd be happy to have me back. I done told Jeramiah to fill my position here and yours, too."

Mattie turned to him with her mouth agape, "You what?" she drew her hand back and slapped her husband soundly on the face. "You had no right to do that," Mattie snapped loudly. "No right at all."

"It's done and I got every right. I'm your husband and *that* gives me the right," he said, rubbing his stinging cheek, "and I signed with an agent up town to sell this house. He'll be over in the mornin' to inspect the property and post a sign."

"You goddamned son-of-a-bitch," Mattie yelled. This is *my* house. *I* bought the land and the lumber with *my* money. You can't sell it out from under me." Tears sprang into her eyes.

"Me and Bump done checked on it, Matilda Grace," Joshua said loudly, shaking his head and backing away from his wife whose eyes blazed with tears of anger and frustration. "This house is mine to do with as I see fit and I decided it's time for you come to Colorado and take up your wifely duties to me."

"Get out of *my* house, Joshua Kirby," Mattie yelled and pointed to the door. "You gave up your rights to my wifely *duties* when you walked out the day of our Emma Sue's funeral." Mattie stomped her booted foot on the freshly polished pine floor. "Get out and if you think for one minute I'm letting any *agents* or anybody else into *my* house you've lost your damned fool mind. Now get out." Mattie picked up a plate and pitched it with all her strength, slinging dishwater, at her retreating husband. "I never want to see your face again so long as I live!" She yelled as Joshua fled out the kitchen door.

The delicate china plate shattered upon the door frame and Mattie slid to the floor weeping uncontrollably. Roxie found her that way when she came rushing in with the basket of laundry resting upon her hip.

"What did that son-of-a-bitch do, Red? Did he hurt you?" Roxie took her sobbing friend into her arms. "What did he say to upset you like this?"

"He's selling my house," Mattie wailed, "and he told Jeramiah to replace me at the office."

"He what?" Roxie asked in confusion as she rocked Mattie, crumpled to her knees in front of the sink. "Calm down, Red and tell me what's going on."

Mattie took a deep breath to calm her weeping. "He came back here because he thought that if he told me he was sorry for walking out on me that I'd fall right into his arms and go off to one of those damned camps in Colorado with him and resume *my wifely duties*."

"Are you foolin' with me? Did he actually say that; your wifely duties?"

"It's *exactly* what he said," Mattie sobbed, "and then he told me he'd stopped in Colorado Springs to tell Jeramiah to replace the both of us because I'd be joining him in the beautiful Colorado mining camps. Can you believe that?" Mattie wailed. "He expected me to follow him back to the mountains, live in a tent in a filthy mining camp and do my wifely duties to him."

"I can believe it," Roxie said calmly. "The son-of-a-bitch has been listening to Will and getting an ear-full about his rights as a husband, I'm certain."

"Yes," she spat, "He said he'd been discussing things with Will and that an agent is coming over tomorrow to see the house and post a sign that the house is for sale." Mattie hiccupped. "How can he do that to me, Roxie? How can he just come down here after he walked out and take away my home and my job?" Mattie pulled herself up to stand at the sink and asked angrily. "What gives him the damned right?"

"You did," Roxie said softly squeezing Mattie's hands in hers, "when you stood with him in front of that preacher and said 'I do'. You gave him the right to make all your decisions."

"I loved him, Roxie," Mattie sobbed. "I loved him so very much."

"I know you did, Red and that's what makes this all so hard to fathom." Roxie stood, lifted up the boiling pot of water, and poured it over the sink of waiting dishes. "I would have expected bullshit like this from Willard Edwards, but never from Joshua Kirby." Roxie set the empty pot down, tested the temperature with her fingers, and pumped a little more cold water into the sink.

"What are we gonna do Rox?" Mattie sobbed as she pulled herself to her feet at the sink. "What are we gonna do without a house or jobs? Are we gonna have to find cribs and go back to the Trade?"

"Back to the Trade, maybe," Roxie mused, "but certainly not in shabby little cribs on Gurley Street."

Chapter 10

May 22, 1879

"What do you think, Red?" Roxie asked, standing before the shell of the three story house on the hill above the main square in Prescott. The structure had been started by a former Territorial Senator who'd been caught in a scandal and forced out of government service. The house, built on three acres with stables, and a coach house with servants' quarters had been a steal at three thousand dollars, but the finish work on the inside, and furnishings would have to be paid for by Roxie.

"Are you sure about this Rox? It's gonna cost a lot of money to finish this big place and you can't call it The Palace because there's already one of those in Prescott."

"We'll think of something else to call it and this is absolutely perfect," Roxie mused, "we can finish it just the way we want it to begin with rather than getting stuck with something that has to be *redone.*" Roxie stared up at the big house with a broad smile on her pale face. "This is perfect, Red. It's what I've always dreamed of. Ophelia would be so jealous. This House is gonna absolutely put The Palace in St. Louis to shame. We have so many plans to make, Red," Roxie said gleefully taking her friend's hands. "We have to pick a name, pick colors for the rooms and buy furniture," Roxie rattled on with exuberance. "I have the money. It's been in the bank for over a year. This house is exactly what the both of us need. Isn't it ever so excitin', Red?"

"It's gonna be a lot of work," Mattie sighed, gazing up at the unpainted gingerbread trim on the big house. How many bedrooms does it have? How many girls are you thinkin'?"

"As it stands now, there are five bedrooms, but we can add two more on the top floor," she said and pointed to the two turrets, "in those attic rooms. I thought we'd make those our personal rooms." Roxie opened the door and stepped inside the unfinished foyer of the big, empty house. It smelled of raw lumber. "I'm thinkin' we should hire at least ten experienced girls who can trade off during their monthlies." Roxie led Mattie through the foyer and into a long room with a fireplace and bookshelves at one end. "This is the parlor and this," she opened a set of double doors that led into another room, "is the private dining room. I think we should make this a private hall with scantily clad dancers doing bawdies for very *special* guests." Roxie grinned and winked at Mattie.

"You've been givin' all of this some careful thought," Mattie said with a grin. Roxie's exuberance was infectious. "Tell me more."

Roxie led Mattie into the kitchen. Mattie could tell the Senator had planned this room with dinner parties and other entertaining in mind. She saw deep sinks with double pumps, a very large cook stove, and bread ovens built into one side of the room's massive fireplace. Mattie had never seen such an impressive kitchen. On one wall, Roxie opened a door to reveal a dumbwaiter to lift trays of food to the upper floors. There was also a large icebox—a very modern convenience for a house in the western territories.

"We're gonna throw the most magnificent parties Prescott, Arizona, has ever seen," Roxie gushed. "I even know who I want to get to cook for us."

"Who?" Mattie asked with a raised red eyebrow.

"Miss Minnie from over at Carson's. I just happen to know she's not happy workin' for that hateful bastard and would jump at the chance to get out of his kitchen."

"Minnie's a good cook," Mattie agreed, bouncing her red curls as she nodded. "I've never understood why she stayed with Matt Carson. He's got to be one of the meanest-mouthed men I've ever known and makes no secret of his dislike for people of color."

"Miss Minnie would be a prize for this kitchen and she can have her own room here," Roxie said, pointing to the room just off the kitchen meant for the cook or butler.

"Where do you plan to house the girls who aren't taking clients?"

"There's a whole suite of rooms above the stables we can use or the ones over the coach house. There's plenty of room here."

"We're not gonna have grooms or stablemen?"

"We can hire men or boys already livin' here in town. We don't have to house them too."

"Makes sense," Mattie agreed. "We should use as many local workers and suppliers as possible. The good folks in town will be much more acceptable of a professional House if we're redistributing the profits back out into the local community."

"The Senator brought up workers to frame this house from Phoenix," Roxie said, nodding. "I know it chapped the hides of the local carpenters. I talked to Virgil Earp the other day when he was up here lookin' to see what lumber might be left lying around. It seems the Senator left owin' the sawmill where Virgil works a big bill."

"Get with Virgil, Rox," Mattie said, picking up on her friend's excitement, "and have him give you a list of good finish carpenters from

90

around town. Remind him that you didn't make the bill for what the Senator ordered, but let him know you'll be buyin' all the finish lumber from his employers and will be using local people to finish the house." Mattie took a deep breath and ran a hand through her loose hair as she thought. "You might ask after furniture builders, as well. We're gonna need several beds, wardrobes, and other things we can't buy from Riley's."

"I'll do that," Roxie said and pulled Mattie toward the broad staircase, leading up to the next floor. "Just look at this." Roxie motioned around a huge open space. "It's a ballroom, Red ... a goddamned ballroom." She pointed to the far end of the expansive room. "We can have a stage built and have a singer like Dora or an orchestra for dancing. Do you think we should build a regular bar and have a saloon up here too?"

Mattie stared at her friend with her eyes wide. "I don't think we should compete with the saloons on Whiskey Row, Rox. We might get away with competing with the crib girls and even to girls with pimps working at The Palace, but those saloon owners can get mean when you start messing with their business."

Roxie looked pensive with a petite finger between her teeth. "You could be right, Red. We can offer liquor to our clients, but we don't need the extra trouble of a full-time saloon with rowdy drunks and fights." She looked around the big room. "We don't need gamblin' tables either. That would really send them on a terror against us down on Whiskey Row if we had Faro tables, roulette wheels, and poker up here."

"Absolutely," Mattie agreed, "we want this House to be a place of refinement and class. Our girls will be the best dressed in Prescott." She gazed around the big room and then down the stairs. "I think we should fill those book shelves next to the fireplace downstairs with books and make certain the girls read them." Mattie began strolling around the big dancefloor, looking up at the high ceiling. "If they can't read, we'll hold classes every day and teach them. This town is full of educated politicians. Our girls have to read the newspaper every morning and be familiar with the current political events so they can hold intelligent conversations with the men who visit. Men who are entertained with conversation will spend more for *other* entertainments."

"They need to be able to do more with their mouths than suck cocks," Roxie said, nodding in agreement. She hugged Mattie with a broad smile on her pale face. "I knew you'd be a great partner in this, Red. We're gonna make a goddamned fortune here."

"It's gonna be a lot of work," Mattie sighed, staring around the big open space. "A lot of work. When do you think we'll be opening for business?"

Roxie took a deep breath. "I don't know for certain, but let's shoot for Independence Day. The town will be full of politicians and they usually put on a big to-do for Independence Day down town. Don't they? We should take advantage of that."

"That's a great idea, Rox, but it gives us less than three months. Do you think we can swing it?"

"Not if we don't get our asses to work," Roxie said as she led her friend up the next flight of stairs to see the existing bedroom spaces.

***

The next six weeks were a flurry of work around the House they'd decided to name the Victoriana after the Queen in England. Mattie wasn't certain Her Majesty would be pleased to hear such a thing, but didn't think they'd have to worry about it.

Virgil Earp made connections for them with good carpenters and in no time at all beautiful windows had been installed, doors hung, and privy closets installed with working plumbing. Parquet tiles of honey-colored oak went down over the pine planks, and wide carved casings went up around the doors and windows. The walls were plastered and sanded smooth before being painted. They painted the parlor a Wedgewood blue and had embossed tin tiles applied to the ceilings. Each room had a color theme. The rooms painted in blue had silver ceilings, those painted in terracotta or rose hues had gold ceiling tiles and those in green had copper ceilings to represent the territory's rich mineral wealth, paying homage to the miners and mine owners whose patronage they hoped to attract to the Victoriana.

As they'd discussed, Roxie and Mattie had stairs built to the attic and had it finished to accommodate their personal bedrooms. Roxie, of course, chose blue and silver for her room while Mattie chose green and copper for hers.

"You sure about this?" Mattie had asked her partner as they watched workmen struggling to carry heavy furniture up the narrow stairs. "Climbing three sets of stairs after a hard day of work isn't gonna be much of a pleasure," she said, grinning at the little blonde in her dusty work dress. "And I doubt customers are gonna want to make the trek. They'll be too worn out to get their cocks hard after climbing all those stairs."

"I don't know about you, Red, but we're management now and I'm goin' for top-dollar. I'm not climbin' those stairs for less than a twenty-dollar gold piece. I'll be the Silver Queen," Roxie laughed, "and you can be the Copper." She waved her little hand around. "This is our palace and I've just crowned us the Queens of Prescott."

"That sounds good to me," Mattie said, but rolled her eyes at her friend's mirth and returned to business. "Do we have all the girls we want now?"

"I'd like a couple more," Roxie sighed, "but we've scoured all the cribs and the hotels in town and hired away the prettiest and brightest of the lot. Do you think we should make a trip down to Phoenix to see if we can find some others down there?"

"No," Mattie said with a slight shake of her red curls, "once word gets around, we'll have experienced girls knocking at *our* door looking for work."

"I thought the same," Roxie agreed and nodded. "How are things goin' with the permits and such?"

Roxie had tasked Mattie with approaching Virgil for his help with the local law commission for permits.

"The bastards at the law commission want a hefty percentage and the availability of any girl at any time," Mattie sighed.

"How hefty?" Roxie asked with a raised eyebrow. "Greedy bastards."

"Virgil says they want ten percent on the girls and fifteen on any liquor we sell and anything we make on gaming tables."

Roxie gave a huff, "Well, they're not gonna be happy when they find out we're not sellin' any liquor here or openin' any tables."

"They figure someone'll come along and make us an offer for a faro table we won't be able to pass on," Mattie sighed.

"Well, they figure wrong. The Victoriana is a quality House. If they want cheap whiskey and crooked card tables, they can take their behinds down to Whiskey Row with the rest of the trash. We offer hot food, hot cunny, clean beds, and good musical entertainment. If we can't make a good living from that, then we should retire."

"Virgil says he'll have our permits as soon as we've hired all our girls and he verifies that none of them have warrants for anything in the Territory."

"Good," Roxie said with a relieved smile. "Can we take them all down to your dressmaker next week to have them measured for their clothes?"

"Mrs. Clayton says she'll have the drapes finished in a few days and will come measure the girls when she delivers them."

Mattie had found Mrs. Clayton through Mr. Riley at the mercantile. He sold her fabric regularly and in turn sold men's shirts, women's, and children's garments Mrs. Clayton made in his store. Mattie had inspected the woman's work and approached her about a commission for drapes, bed coverlets, and pillows for the Victoriana.

After meeting the miner's widow and realizing she fed her four children with what she made from her seamstress work, Mattie had returned to the mercantile, purchased one of those new mechanical sewing machines, and presented it to the woman along with a list of the items they needed and a line of credit with Riley for the fabric. Later, she'd broached the subject of dressing the women at the Victoriana and was very pleased when the seamstress had enthusiastically agreed without a hint of reservation.

"I don't know what to say, Mrs. Kirby," said the pale, thin woman with stringy brown hair. "A commission like this will feed me and my children for a year. I don't know what to say except thank you for considering me for the work."

"Don't be silly, Mrs. Clayton. I'm the one who should be thankful," Mattie said and blushed. "Not many would consider sewing for whores or a whore house."

"There's plenty of high-minded holier-than-thou fools in this town, Mrs. Kirby and I don't count myself amongst them." She took Mattie's hand. "I have four children to feed and I've only got one good way of making money. I'm too old to hire on at your fine House," she said with a sheepish grin, "but in my younger days I danced on a boat out of New Orleans. I met my man on that boat and if most of those fine church women knew it, they'd shun me and not buy my clothes for their precious children."

"Your secret is safe with me," Mattie said with an impish grin. "I'm not on conversational terms with any of them myself."

"You're the better for it," Mrs. Clayton said returning Mattie's grin.

Furniture for the Victoriana had been commissioned with two shops and began arriving soon after the paint on the plastered walls had dried. Each bedroom had a bed, a wardrobe, a bedside table, and a vanity with a bench. Framed mirrors hung over each vanity, as well as in the privy closets. They purchased mattresses and pillows from the mercantile along with lamps bearing bright, colorful shades. Fixtures had been installed in each ceiling with the anticipation of gas soon to be available in the town for residential lighting. Huge gas chandeliers were hung in the foyer and the ballroom. When lit, the House would fairly sparkle.

Chapter 11

June 2, 1879

Mattie stood folding the last of her things into her cases to carry out to the wagon and haul to the Victoriana. They wouldn't have any use for flowery cotton curtains or the little potbelly stove, but she'd be damned if she'd leave one thing in the house she'd made or paid for. It could all rot in the basement of the Victoriana for all Mattie cared, but she'd probably end up sending a good bit of it to people around town she knew who could use it.

"Is that the last of it Mrs. Kirby?" Jessie Hammond asked as he pumped some cold water into a cup. He'd helped her load furniture and boxes. Although the morning had begun cool with a light breeze, the afternoon had turned warm with bright sun and clear skies.

"This is it, Jessie," she said as she carried the buckled leather case from the bedroom. "Did you get all the peaches?"

"Yes, ma'am and I picked all the cucumbers before pullin' up the plants." He gave her a perplexed grin. "I still don't quite understand why you wanted me to rip up the garden after all the work we put into plantin' and tendin' it all these months."

Mattie handed him the case of curtains. "You're still young, Jessie. I'm sure when you're older and have a wife you'll understand it all just fine." She smiled. "Why don't you take the wagon up to your momma's and tell her she can have anything off it she needs then haul the rest of it up to the Victoriana and put it down in the basement."

"Yes ma'am," he said eagerly. "Momma can use that bed from Miss Roxie's room I know for certain and the cook stove. Ours smokes somethin' fierce and is a might rusted through."

"Take it then with my blessings for all your hard work," Mattie said, smiling at the tall, slender young man.

"Thank you, ma'am," he said with a broad smile on his freckled face and rushed out the kitchen door and across the back porch.

Mattie looked up when she heard boot steps on the porch and wondered what the boy had forgotten. Her face fell when she saw that it wasn't Jessie Hammond, but Joshua Kirby walking into the empty kitchen.

"Hello Mattie," he said softly as he gazed around the empty room. His face turned dark when he saw the bare windows and the empty spot where the stove had once stood. "You took down the curtains *and* the stove? That little gal went on and on about how much she liked them curtains and her husband thought he was buyin' a house with a cook stove," Joshua said, stamping his foot on the wood planked floor.

"Well, won't they just be surprised," Mattie snapped, "I made those curtains and I bought the stoves. None of *that* was yours to sell."

Mattie watched Joshua's face blaze red before he turned to stare out the back door. "What happened to the garden?" He demanded. "And the fruit on the trees?"

"I gave it all to the Hammonds," Mattie said coolly. "Did you honestly think I was gonna leave the garden I sweated over to grow for your new tenants to enjoy? I may have been fool enough to marry the likes of you, Joshua Kirby, but I'm not fool enough to leave behind one single thing I spent *my* time and sweat on for another damned woman and *her* man to enjoy."

"I never figured you for a mean-spirited woman, Matilda Grace. That little gal and her husband are expectin' a baby in the fall and thought on havin' a place with a thrivin' garden, a cook stove, and curtains on the windows." He shook his head and shrugged his wide shoulders. "I might have to give them some of their money back for this."

"If you think that's gonna go breakin' my heart any," she huffed, "then you have another thing comin'. Or did you plan on refunding me the money I used to build and furnish this place?" Mattie watched his eyes go wide and his mouth fall open. "Yah, I didn't think so."

He glowered at her across the room. "Bump said that money became legally mine as soon as I put that ring on your finger and you took my name. I don't have to give you nothin' and because you decided to steal them curtains and the stoves I'm probably gonna have to give part of it back to that young couple."

Mattie shrugged her shoulders and returned his scowl. "I made the curtains, planted the garden, tended the fruit, and paid for the stoves."

"You're as mean-spirited a bitch as any whore I've ever known, Matilda Grace," Joshua snarled. "I don't know what good I ever seen in ya 'cept what's between your legs." Joshua glared at her. "You should have left the curtains and the garden."

"And if they'd wanted a cook and gardener? Should I have stayed and done that, as well, Joshua?"

"You're just bein' silly now," he sighed. "Nobody would have expected that."

"And I never expected to be thrown out of *my* house after you left me alone in it, but here we are." Mattie stormed past his bulk and out the door. She made her way to the buggy and climbed in. "If I never see your face again, Joshua, it will be too damned soon." Mattie didn't know if he could hear her and didn't really care. She flicked the reins and her horse began moving toward the street, where a young couple in a newer buggy were turning into the lane toward the little yellow house trimmed in white with a picket fence around the yard and garden area.

May god grant you the peace and happiness I hoped for there, but never had.

Tears streaked Mattie's face when she entered the kitchen of the Victoriana to find Roxie sitting at the small round oak table that had until recently graced Mattie's other kitchen.

"What's wrong, Red?" Roxie asked, noting her friend's eyes. "What happened?"

Mattie took a deep breath. "Oh nothing, I just ran into Joshua at the house is all."

"I suppose that would do it." Roxie stood and poured Mattie a cup of coffee. "What did the son-of-a-bitch say to get you so riled up?"

"He told me I was a mean-spirited bitch of a whore for taking down the curtains and giving the furniture and peaches to Mrs. Hammond."

"Well," Roxie said, grinning, "you *are* a whore, but I never knew you to be mean-spirited."

"He didn't like it much that I had Jamie pick the peaches off the trees and pull up the garden."

"You didn't?" Roxie gasped wide-eyed. "Well, maybe you're a little mean-spirited after all. You didn't poison the well too, did you?"

"No, I didn't think about that," she admitted, furrowing her brow and trying to hold back the grin tugging at the corners of her mouth.

"Then you're not as mean-spirited as I would have been." Roxie poured a splash of Tennessee whiskey into each of their cups. "Hell, I burned *my* house to the ground up in Forestville. Remember?"

"That I do," Mattie said and took a sip of her coffee. "I suppose we're both just mean-spirited whores after all."

"I suppose we are," Roxie sighed. "You going to get your things out of the office in the morning now that you've cleaned out the house?"

"Yah," Mattie sighed sadly, "I suppose I'd better. The new man will be there to start soon."

***

The following morning, dressed conservatively in high-collared dresses Mattie and Roxie walked to the office of Harvey & Edwards with an empty box under each of their arms. Mattie unlocked the door with her brass key and led Roxie inside.

"Rox, you box up all the personal stationary, pens, and inks and I'll take the things off the walls and windows." Mattie cleared a place on her desk and set the wooden box atop it. She popped the wooden dowel from its holder and slid the lace curtains off. Bright sunlight streamed into the dark room.

"You're takin' the curtains?" Roxie said with a mischievous giggle.

"Damned right I am," Mattie huffed. "When Josh and I got here this place was as bare as a bone gnawed by a wolf. I made and put up these curtains, I found the pictures for the walls, and the spittoons as well. I paid for them and if Jeramiah Harvey wants to argue the point, he's welcome to, but I have the receipts from Riley's."

"I'm sure you do, Red. You're the most efficient business woman I've ever known and Jeramiah knows it, too," Roxie said as she took stationary with Mattie's name on it from a drawer to stack into the box upon her desk. "He'll be hard pressed to find a *man* any better."

As Mattie folded curtains into her box, the door opened and a heavy-set man wearing a plaid wool waistcoat walked in followed by Mr. Grady from the telegraph office.

"Hello, Mrs. Kirby," the telegrapher said smugly, "this is my brother … your new boss." He glanced at Roxie and sneered, "I don't believe your services will be required any longer, madam; you can go." He held the door open dismissing Roxie, who ignored him and continued filling her box. "What are you doing to the office, Mrs. Kirby?"

"I'm collecting *my* belongings so the new man can make it his own." She glared at the skinny telegrapher. "Neither Miss North nor I are employed by Harvey & Edwards any longer. We'll be out of your way in a few minutes, Mr. Grady. The office will be yours to do with as you please."

"But …" stammered the portly man, his eyes wide with surprise as he turned to his brother, "but I thought she was supposed to stay and be my personal assistant."

"You mean," Roxie huffed from her desk, "that you thought she was gonna stay and do the job *for* you?"

"We simply assumed," said the thin Grady brother, "that Mrs. Kirby would continue on in her capacity as … as an assistant to my brother until he got familiar with the running of the place."

"If you *need* an assistant to do this job, Mr. Grady, you'll have to take it up with Jeramiah Harvey. I don't work for Harvey and Edwards any longer." Mattie took down a color print of a steaming locomotive framed in brass and propped it gently into the box.

"But how am I supposed to figure out what I need to know?" the portly brother asked.

"Just like I did when I got here, Mr. Grady," Mattie sighed, "just like I did. All the files are in that cabinet there with the names of suppliers and their current contracts." She handed him the key to the office.

Roxie dropped a hand full of pens into her box. "And don't forget to read that fat file with the newspaper clippin's about the trial of Martin Rowe and how he got that long prison sentence for cheatin' Mr. Harvey with bogus supply contracts and such." She winked at Mattie. "It's real lively readin'." She picked up her box, walked past the two men, who stood staring open-mouthed around the now very plain-looking office, and followed Mattie out the door.

Chapter 12

July 4, 1879

The girls hired, the house furnished, and the entertainment booked, The Victoriana's grand-opening arrived with fireworks exploding overhead and an orchestra playing chamber music in the ballroom upstairs. Roxie, wearing a brilliant blue sleeveless gown trimmed in bright white lace stood in the dazzling foyer greeting guests as they arrived. Nineteen-year-old Jessie Hammond had been fitted with a black wool waistcoat and acted as doorman for the evening.

All the girls were dressed in elegant evening gowns, sparkling with multitudes of clear beads sewn onto the fabrics to catch the light from the chandeliers as they moved. Mattie dressed in daffodil yellow dazzled the eye with her bright red curls piled upon her head decorated with a white ostrich plume. She wore white opera gloves that reached to her elbows and narrow white lace accentuated the low neckline of her gown, showing off her bulging creamy bosoms.

"Isn't it wonderful?" Roxie whispered nervously to Mattie as they watched a senator escort a lady he'd introduced as his niece up the stairs to the ballroom. "I never realized the government officials here in Prescott had so many nieces."

"Indeed," Mattie agreed with a giggle. "The clergy as well."

Another young man in black came by carrying a silver tray with tiny sandwiches and Mattie grabbed one. She popped it into her mouth and chewed quickly. She washed it down with a sip of sweet pink wine from her long-stemmed crystal glass.

The house smelled of roses from the bunches filling vases around the rooms and of meat roasting in the kitchen. That room had been abuzz with activity for days. Miss Minnie had brought in her daughter Mary and her granddaughter Elsie to help with the preparations. Fresh bread had been baking for two days along with tiny fruit tarts, and an assortment of meats. Much of the meat had also been cooked into tiny bite-size crusts to be passed around on trays for the guests to enjoy, while the rest would be sent up on trays to fill the buffet in the ballroom.

Mattie and Roxie had advertised the grand-opening of The Victoriana in the newspaper as a new entertainment venue where people could come and enjoy stage performances, dance to an orchestra, and dine at the free buffet. Nobody in town was fooled. They all knew the Victoriana was a house of ill-repute, but would not miss the opportunity to dance and dine for free.

Many wanted to get a look at the inside of the big house on the hill that had been the talk of the town for months with the bustle of workmen and influx of fixtures and furnishings. None wanted to say they'd missed out on the excitement of the Independence Day festivities and few in town did.

By eight o'clock the dancefloor in the ballroom had filled and the parlor buzzed with laughter and frivolity. The only event marring the night was the drunken arrival of a prominent rancher John Dewey and his friend Alan Ramsay who owned a gold mine some miles southwest of Prescott.

They were dressed for the occasion in their best suits, but wreaked of alcohol and cigars from a day of Independence Day entertainments in the saloons and gambling houses on Whiskey Row.

"We want a whore," bellowed John Dewey as he burst past Jessie at the door. "This is a whorehouse, isn't it? We want us a whore."

"Gentlemen," Roxie said in her sweetest southern drawl, "The Victoriana isn't officially open for business tonight. This is just a night to introduce us to the community." She smiled sweetly and gestured toward the stairs. "The girls are all upstairs dancin', if you'd like to go up and introduce yourselves. There is a free buffet if you're hungry and the boys are passin' around drinks."

John Dewey, a big man, grabbed Roxie by the shoulder and spun her slight frame around to face him. He reached out and began touching the pale bosom mounding above the low neckline of her blue gown. "I like you," he said, leering down at Roxie's chest. "What you think about this one, Al?" He lifted a finger to Roxie's rouged lips and laughed. "Won't these look nice wrapped around my cock?"

Alan Ramsay grinned nervously at Roxie. He was a handsome man and filled out his expensive suit nicely. "That they would, John, but the lady says they aren't taking customers tonight. Maybe we should just go on over to The Palace and find Joanna. Her lips feel as nice as any."

"You'll not find Joanna at the Palace," Roxie said. "She works here now and is upstairs dancing along with the other girls."

John Dewey's eyes gazed up the wide staircase with a frown. "Damn, do you have all the women in town dancing up there?" He stormed. "And you aren't letting any of them fuck tonight?"

"Sir," Roxie said sweetly as she reached into the blue velvet bag dangling from her wrist, "here are two of my cards. If you'll bring these back with you after we've opened for business and present them at the door, you may have your choice of women for an hour on the house."

Each man took a card from her gloved hand and Ramsay nudged his big friend. "Come on John, let's go up and see who else they have on their payroll and have a look at that spread of free food." He tugged the big man by the elbow toward the stairway. Roxie watched them stumble up the carpeted stairs, laughing drunkenly as they went. Ramsay turned and gave Roxie a quick wink and a smile as he herded his friend up the stairs.

"I'm sorry, Miss Roxie," Jessie said nervously, "I tried to stop them from coming in, but they just busted right past me."

"It's alright, Jessie. Those are important men in this area and we can't afford to turn away their future business."

"Yes ma'am," he mumbled, "thank you ma'am." He bumped into Mattie on his way back to the door.

"Is everything alright?" Mattie asked, watching the young man walk slump-shouldered back to the door.

"Yes, just some drunken men looking to take advantage of the House."

"Aren't they all?" Mattie sighed.

"How are things going upstairs?"

"Just fine. Minnie has food running up that pulley cart on a regular basis, the first two barrels of wine have been emptied, and the orchestra is on their second round of their sheet music. Everything is going just fine."

"And the girls? How are they gettin' on?" Roxie asked. "Are they conducting themselves like genteel ladies or a bunch of filthy whores from Whiskey Row let loose in a fine house?"

"The girls are conducting themselves very nicely," Mattie said with a satisfied smile, patting Roxie's shoulder reassuringly. "They look beautiful and I haven't heard one *fuck* or *cock-sucker* from any of them."

"That's a relief," Roxie sighed. "I was worried. I want the people here to see elegant, refined women and not common street whores or dancehall women." They'd given all the girls strong warnings to watch their manners and their language, but Roxie knew rough women couldn't be trusted to mind their tongues after a few drinks.

"We've hired the best of the best in Prescott, Rox. They know they've been given an opportunity here and won't do anything to lose it." Mattie hugged her friend close as they stood in the middle of the brightly lit parlor. "Don't worry. This is going to be a night Prescott is going to be talking about for years to come." A young man dressed in black came by with a tray and Mattie scooped a hand-full of little meat pies from it. "Here Rox, eat something or you're going to fall over in a nervous faint."

Roxie took two of the savory little pies and popped one into her mouth. "Umm ..." She sighed as she chewed the minced beef cooked with onions, garlic, and carrots in brown gravy and baked into the tiny, flakey pie crust, "Miss Minnie is one hell of a cook, Red. We are damned lucky to have her."

"Language," Mattie chided with a broad smile as she bit into a pie as well. "I'll have to wash your mouth out if I hear another curse word come out of it. This is a quality House filled with quality women not a common crib down on Whiskey Row filled with common, foul-mouthed women."

"That it is, and I thank you for reminding me outside the hearing of our employees lest they think me a terrible hypocrite."

Another couple in evening dress walked in and Mattie greeted them. Roxie shook their hands and sent them up the stairs to enjoy the music, food, and drink. She walked back to Mattie with a smile on her pretty face.

"Does Jessie seem alright to you?" Mattie asked her petite friend. "He won't look me in the eye tonight."

"I think he's just figured out what we're about here," Roxie said with a sheepish grin.

"Oh my," Mattie sighed and walked through the opened door and out onto the porch where the young man stood leaning against the porch railing as he waited for more people to arrive.

"What do you think about the Victoriana?" Mattie asked as she stepped beside him.

"It's a right fine place, Mrs. Kirby," he said, edging away from her nervously.

"But you don't approve."

"It's not my place to approve or disapprove, Mrs. Kirby, ma'am."

"But you understand what will be going on here?" Mattie asked uneasily.

"Well ... of course I ..." he stammered and Mattie watched as his cheeks turned bright red, "I mean, yes, I know what goes on in a cathouse. I'm not daft ... or a vir ... I know," he finally said resolutely and Mattie saw crimson flood his cheeks in the light from the chandelier in the foyer.

Mattie grinned in the flickering shadows cast by the lamps strung around the big porch. "Of course, you do. If you're not comfortable working here in the house, you can work with the boys in the stables or with the gardeners."

Jessie ran a hand over the fine soft wool of his waistcoat and fingered one of the silver buttons. "Oh no, ma'am, I like workin' here in the house just fine." He stood up straighter and looked Mattie in the eye. "And it's not my place to pass judgement on anything or anyone here. I appreciate you giving me the opportunity to earn extra money to help out my momma." He took a deep breath. "She's gone and got herself with child again. With another mouth to feed she'll need everything I can put by."

"Jessie, you're her son, not her husband," Mattie said sternly to the youth. "Why isn't your father out looking for extra work to feed *his* children?"

"Pa works hard in the fields," Jessie said, defending his father. "He has fifty acres to tend and a herd of a hundred cattle." He took another breath and stared up at the ceiling of the porch. "I just wish he'd visit places like this rather than getting another baby on Momma when she can hardly deal with the ones she has now."

It eased Mattie's mind that Jessie Hammond understood exactly what would be going on at The Victoriana and she couldn't help but giggle. She took the boy's hand into hers. "Have you spoken to your father about it?"

"It's not my place ..." he began.

"Then it's not your place to be expected to support his get," Mattie snapped. "You're a good boy, Jessie, but you should be saving your money for the time when you have a girl of your own with *your* child in her belly to provide for." Mattie patted his hand. "If you're old enough to be expected to support your family, you're old enough to talk to your father about *his* responsibilities. If he doesn't like it," Mattie continued, "there is always a place for you here."

Jessie looked over with his brown eyes wide. "Thank you, Mrs. Kirby, ma'am, but I can't leave my momma or my brothers and sisters. I'll stay on the farm," he sighed heavily, "but I'm goin' to have that talk with Pa about keeping his cock outa Momma. She's getting' too old to be carrying babies in her belly. I fear for her every time the pains start comin' on." His voice trailed off.

"There are herbs I can give her to keep her from getting with child," Mattie told the boy. "I'll go have a talk with her."

"I'd surely appreciate that ma'am." He smiled sadly at Mattie and then looked up as another carriage came up the drive. "I guess we'd better get back to work. I never knew there were so many fancy buggies in Prescott."

"There are lots of fancy men in Prescott, Jessie," Mattie said smiling out at the oncoming buggy, "and fancy men like their fancy buggies."

"I suppose you're right, ma'am," he sighed and grinned. "I suppose you're right."

Chapter 13

July 13, 1879

The opening of the Victoriana had been a rousing success. The following day the newspaper gave them a splendid review, touting the beauty of the building and the owners and hostesses, as well as the wonderful food and liquid libations. The writer proclaimed the evening marvelous and said he looked forward to attending more social engagements there.

"You have to read this, Red?" Roxie exclaimed as Mattie trudged into the kitchen the next morning in her dressing gown. She shoved the newspaper into Mattie's hand as the redhead sat and Minnie carried a steaming pot of coffee to set upon the table.

"Can I make you some breakfast, Miss Mattie?" Minnie asked as she poured coffee into a delicate porcelain cup.

"Do you have any of those berry tarts left?" Mattie asked before picking up her steaming cup.

"I think there might be a few left," Minnie said rolling her big brown eyes. "That bunch last night didn't leave much behind. I ain't never seen people eat like them fancy-dressed fools last night and none of them looked like they been missin' many meals neither."

"The food was free," Roxie snorted. "You offer free food to a bunch of politicians and they'll scoop up everything but the floor boards."

"I can attest to that," Minnie said, shaking her head with a chuckle as she filled a small plate with tarts and set them on the table in front of Mattie. "Elsie said she seen some of them men stuffing the pockets of them big coats with meat pies on their way out."

"You're a good cook, Minnie," Mattie said as she bit into one of the berry-filled tarts, "they probably never tasted the like."

"Thank you, Miss Mattie, but I was just doin' what you fine ladies pay me to do." She hesitated a moment before continuing. "I appreciate you hirin' Mary and Elsie on for the doin's, as well. If you're planin' on big parties like that in the future might I be so bold as to take leave to have them help me again? Ol' Carson let them both go down to the restaurant after I left, thinkin' I'd come crawlin' back to him, but I won't do that." Minnie stood with her gnarled brown hands on her hips shaking her kerchiefed head.

Mattie looked up from the newspaper. "Why didn't you mention that before, Minnie?" She gazed over at Roxie who was adding a splash of Tennessee whiskey to her cup of coffee.

"We haven't hired a laundress or house girl yet," Roxie said, turning to Mary and Elsie, who stood at the sinks washing and drying crystal glasses from the night before, "Mary, would you and Elsie mind doin' a bit of washin' and housekeepin' around here?"

"Not at all, Miss Roxie, ma'am," the younger Negro woman said, twisting her hands in her white cotton apron.

Minnie took a deep breath. "Would it be too much for me to ask that they be allowed to share my room here? It's a long walk from the place they be stayin' now and if they was stayin' here on the property they could get an earlier start on their chores and such."

"There are three bedrooms over the stable," Mattie offered and nodded toward the building out back. "You can all have rooms of your own."

Roxie saw tears fill the old Negro woman's eyes. "You don't have to be doin' that, Miss Roxie. Me and my girls can share this here room off the kitchen here. It'll hold three cots easy. It's all we need and you'll be needin' them rooms over the stables for your extra women."

"Don't be ridiculous," Roxie said as she stood and took the woman's trembling brown hand. "If it weren't for you and your amazing girls, last night wouldn't have been near the success it was. You, Mary, and Elsie are important to the Victoriana. We want you to be happy and comfortable."

"That's right," Mattie said, thumping the newspaper, "it says so right here. We can put two beds in this room off the kitchen for the girls to use during their monthlies and," she hesitated, thinking, "well, we'll work things out for the others. This is a big house. We'll find room for them all."

"Yes, we will," Roxie said. "Don't you worry about it. We'll have Jessie take Mary and Elsie out in the buckboard to pick up their things to bring back here and y'all can move into the rooms over the stables. We can put the extra girls up in the rooms over the carriage house. We were going to hire a groom from town anyhow."

Mattie found the day after the grand opening taxing and sat with a book in the parlor, enjoying a breeze coming through the open window. Roxie joined her, still in her blue dressing gown with her blonde waves hanging loose over her shoulders.

"What did you think, Red? How did it go?"

"I think it went just fine, Rox," Mattie sighed and put her book on the table beside the chair. "Are we opening the doors for actual business tonight?"

"At five sharp," Roxie said exuberantly. "Minnie and her girls should have the place back in order by then and our girls will be rested and ready to go."

Two women walked through the parlor with cups of coffee in their hands and mounted the stairs.

"How do you think the girls were received?" Roxie asked, watching the trailing tails of dressing gowns disappear up the wide stairs. "We only have seven. We should be lookin' for more."

"I thought we decided to wait and let them come to us," Mattie sighed. This had been a bone of contention for the past several weeks between the two friends. Roxie was nervous about having enough women to staff the Victoriana, while Mattie thought they had enough to get the place going. She didn't think they needed to worry about looking for other women until they had an established client base.

"I know," Roxie said, leafing through a periodical with color plates of stylish dresses and hats, but what if five of the seven all get their monthly at the same time?"

Mattie rolled her eyes. "You think that's likely to happen?"

"It happens," Roxie snorted. "I saw it at one of the houses I worked at in New Orleans. There were ten gals workin' and seven of us got our monthly at the same time. Madam Ophelia had to take clients," she said with a grin.

"Well, when you and I have to start taking clients because all the girls are suffering their curses," Mattie said with a chuckle, "then we'll go out looking for more girls."

The clock on the mantle chimed eleven as Mattie emptied her coffee cup. She stood and stretched. "I think I need a little air to clear my head. I have a basket of things that I need to take up to Mrs. Clayton for altering. Do you want to go with me?"

Roxie tossed the periodical on the table and stood. "Might as well," she said glancing out the window. "It looks like a pretty day for a drive." Mary came in to pick up their empty coffee cups and Roxie asked her to have Jessie hitch up the buggy.

Wearing light cotton day dresses, they drove the buggy to Mrs. Clayton's and dropped off the basket of dresses to be altered along with some loaves of bread that hadn't been eaten the night before. Mattie was certain Mrs. Clayton's boys wouldn't allow them to get stale.

Mrs. Clayton's small farm was located a few miles north of Prescott in the rolling hills bordering the windswept desert of the Chino Valley where Chinese mine laborers lived with their families in abject poverty.

"For the life of me," Roxie said, holding her straw bonnet in place as the wind gusted from the mountains across their path, "I don't know how anyone can live up here with all this wind and dust."

"It's only bad in the summer. In the spring it's green and alive with game. Joshua told me he hunted elk and deer out here."

"Slow down, Red," Roxie said, grabbing Mattie's arm and pointing to something in the road ahead. "What's that there? Is it an injured animal?"

Mattie pulled on the reins to slow the buggy and approached the thing sprawled half in the dusty road and half in the tall swaying grasses. She yanked hard as they got close to stop her horse. "Oh my god, it's a girl," she gasped and jumped from the buggy. She rushed to the prone naked form in the dust with Roxie close behind. "It's just a girl, Rox, and look at her," Mattie said as she knelt beside the naked body. "She's been beaten bloody. Get me the canteen from the buggy and the blanket from the back."

Roxie ran back to the buggy while Mattie laid her fingers on the girl's dirty neck to feel for a pulse. She felt a faint one and took the canteen Roxie offered. "She's alive, but barely," Mattie said and put the canteen to the girl's parched, dry lips. The girl began to moan when Mattie lifted her head and her bruised green eyes fluttered open.

"Try to drink this," Mattie said softly and tipped the canteen up until water began to run out and down the girl's dirty chin. It made tracks down her throat through the blood and grime. She gulped the cool water and Mattie had to pull the canteen away, fearing she'd choke or take too much too quick and throw it all back up.

Roxie spread the light woolen blanket they kept folded in the buggy over the girl. "What's your name, Sugar, and what are you doin' out here like *this*?"

The girl tried to sit up, rising on her skinned elbows to stare frantically around. "Help me," she gasped, "please help me."

"Of course, we'll help you, Sugar," Roxie said as she helped the emaciated girl to sit, "but who the hell are you and what are you doin' out here on the road naked as the day you were born?"

Tears began to run down the girl's sunken cheeks. "Me name is Moira," she said with a strong Irish accent. "Where am I?" She asked weakly and pulled to blanket up around her throat, clutching it with thin talon-like fingers. She put one hand up to shield her eyes from the bright July sun. "I don't know where I am."

Mattie took the arm gently to examine the red welts around the wrist. "This girl's been in shackles," Mattie whispered to Roxie. "Do you think she's an escaped criminal?"

"Well, she *is* Irish," Roxie said, glancing down at the dazed girl, "most of them *are*."

"Oh, Rox," Mattie chided softly, "look at her. Would the authorities keep their prisoners naked?"

Moira reached for the canteen tentatively and Mattie gave it to her. "Drink slow or you'll get sick all over yourself."

Moira took the canteen, but did as she was told and drank slowly with her eyes closed.

"How did you get here, Moira?" Mattie asked. "We were just through here two hours ago and you weren't here."

The canteen came away from her lips and Moira used the back of her hand to wipe her mouth. "I saw you," she said. "I was crossin' through that pasture there." She pointed to the field of tall grass to their right. "I knew you wasn't dem for ya was a comin' from the wrong direction, but I was afeared and I hid." She clutched at the blanket. "And I didn't have no clothes on. I waited til ye passed and came on out to the road, but got all fuzzy-headed."

"Typical Irish," Roxie mumbled.

Mattie ignored her friend. "Where were you coming *from* and how did you get those marks on your wrist? Were you in jail?"

Tears began to run down her face again. "Not in jail, but aye, a prisoner," she sobbed.

Roxie took her kerchief from her bag and wiped the girl's swollen face. Beneath the grime she saw what would be a very pretty girl once the bruises faded and the scratches healed. "Tell us what happened to you, Sugar. Who was keepin' you prisoner."

"Deir names be Harley and Pete," she hiccupped. "Dey got me an' t'other girls in Chicago. Dey told our Das an' Mas dey'd take us west to find rich husbands in the goldfields in Colorado." More tears rushed down Moira's face. "Me ma is gonna be so disappointed in me," she sobbed.

"But there were no rich husbands waiting?" Roxie said and brushed the girl's matted auburn hair from her face.

"Oh, dere were husbands aplenty," Moira spat, "but dey were already other women's husbands."

"How long ago did you leave Chicago?" Mattie asked, "And how many girls were with you?"

Moira took a deep, cleansing breath and wiped her eyes again. "We left Chicago on May Day after Da gave Harley and Pete a hundred dollars for me dowry and food for me passage west. It was all the money Da had," she sobbed. "Some of the girl's parents even borrowed money from shylocks to pay deir passages."

"And from the looks of ya," Roxie said, "they didn't feed you very much."

The girls face turned a deep red. "Harley told us de best food came from men's cocks and if we didn't want t' go hungry we'd learn t' milk 'em wid our mouds." She fell sobbing into Roxie's arms.

Roxie held the girl close and patted her heaving shoulders. "It's alright, Sugar," she cooed softly.

"But 'tis not alright," Moira sobbed. "I'm a sinful wanton now and God will condemn me to Hell for the wickedness I've done."

"Don't be silly," Mattie said. "You didn't do any of the things you did because you *wanted* to. God doesn't condemn girls to Hell who've been forced."

Moira glanced at her suspicious. "He doesn't?"

"Of course, he doesn't," Roxie confirmed. "There are plenty of churches in Prescott. I'm sure we can find you a priest to hear your confession and absolve you."

The girl suddenly looked faint. "I couldn't possibly tell a priest about all de …" She swooned into Roxie's arms.

Mattie felt at her throat again. "She's just fainted. She needs food. God only knows when she last had a proper meal." She wet Roxie's kerchief and gently cleaned Moira's face. "Pretty, isn't she?"

"Yes, poor thing." Roxie folded back the blanket so Mattie could wipe the blood and grime from Moira's neck, shoulders, and chest. "What are we gonna do with her?"

"Take her back to the Victoriana and get some food into her to begin with. Do you think you can help me lift her up into the buggy?"

"I'm sure we can manage it," Roxie said, but began staring down the road in the direction of Mrs. Clayton's. "Do you think that Harley and Pete are on her trail? She sure seemed to be afraid of them."

"Look at her," Mattie shrugged, "They've starved and beaten her for months and forced her to couple with strangers. If we could figure out where she ran *from* we might be able to get a better idea of where her handlers might be. If there's just two of them and they've got several girls to look after, they might just cut their losses and let her go."

Roxie stared across the field Moira said she'd come across. "If she was coming from that direction, they probably had their cat wagon parked over at Fort Whipple, selling the girls' cunny to the soldiers there."

They got Moira to her feet and helped her into the buggy. The two women got in on either side of her and tucked the blanket around her frail, shivering body.

"Were you at the fort, Moira?" Mattie asked as she flicked the reins to put the horse in motion again. "Is that where the bastards had you?"

"Aye," Moira said. "We've been camped dere for dree days."

"And you think they'll come looking for you?" Roxie asked as she reached into her bag and took out her silver flask.

"Dey always come," Moira said, taking a deep shivering breath. "Harley likes to hunt down the girls who run. He likes to punish us." Roxie felt the girl shudder. "It pleasures him to beat us and he … has a list of consequences."

"Consequences?" Roxie said, putting the flask to Moira's lips. "What kind of *consequences*?"

Moira gulped down the strong whiskey and then handed the flask back to Roxie. "Dank ye, ma'am." Moira wiped her face with the back of her hand. "The first time ye run away de consequence 'tis a beating and …" she closed her eyes and gulped. "And training in de dings some men like dat are painful." Moira shifted her behind in the seat. "De second time de consequence 'tis de beating, more training, and your clothes and shoes are taken away." Moira lifted one of her blood-encrusted feet. "He chains ye t' de back o' de wagon and makes ye walk naked and widout shoes for a whole day and sometimes twa."

"And when you run away a third time?" Roxie asked, her face red with rage at the unknown Harley. "What is the consequence for that?"

"Only one oder girl ever ran away a dird time," Moira said softly. "We were in de desert east of here and Rachel got up to relieve herself in the night and never came back." She took a deep breath before continuing her story. "Harley went out after her de next mornin' and didn't come back until de next evenin'. De followin' day we drove until about noon and den Harley hauled us all out of the wagon and marched us over to a gully where …" she began to sob, "where Rachel's body was laid out in de bloody sand. He'd beat and used her, then broke bod her legs and staked her out and left her dere naked."

Moira's body shook with her pitiful sobs and Roxie put her arms protectively around the girl's shoulders. "De coyotes had come for 'er in de night," Moira sobbed bitterly in Roxie's arms. "Dey'd chewed up her legs and ripped open her belly." The girl buried her face in Roxie's shoulder. "'Twas awful and Harley said dat's what happened to lazy cunnies who shirked deir duties and tried to run away a dird time."

They rode on into town with the girl tucked into Roxie's arms, sleeping with soft whimpers from time to time.

"Fucking cat wagon pimps," Roxie snarled. "They are the lowest of the low. Not only do they steal these poor girls, but they get their ignorant parents to pay them for the privilege."

Mattie shook her head as the horse brought them into town. "It's a bad business, that's for certain." She glanced over at the girl sleeping in Roxie's arms. "She'll be safe with us at the Victoriana and after we've put a few pounds on her we can send her back to Chicago if she wants to go home."

"She won't want to go," Roxie assured her. "She won't be able to face her family even if a damned priest *will* absolve her."

"How do you know?" Mattie asked as they passed by the cribs on Whiskey Row. She saw Mr. Grady walking down the sidewalk and used the reins to urge the horse along a little faster.

"I was raised Catholic and after what happened to me in Birmingham at my aunt and uncle's," Roxie said with a long sigh and a shrug of her shoulders. "I couldn't go home and face mine. I went to New Orleans and ... well, you know the rest. This girl won't want to go back and face her Irish Catholic family in Chicago." Roxie bent and kissed the auburn hair of the girl breathing softly at her breast.

Chapter 14

August 3, 1879

Moira O'Malley settled in at the Victoriana and within a few weeks of eating Miss Minnie's hearty cooking began to fill out into a beautiful young woman. She told them she'd just turned nineteen the month before. Roxie saw to her recuperation like a mother hen with a sickly chick, making certain the pretty Irish girl ate plenty and regularly, trimming and styling her beautiful auburn curls, and outfitting her with a complete wardrobe of stylish, but conservative clothes.

As they sat having tea in the parlor, looking at fabric samples, Moira cleared her throat and said to Roxie pointedly, "You and Miss Mattie are just like Harley and Pete, aren't you?"

Her tone took them both by surprise. Roxie turned paler than normal and coughed up the tea she'd just swallowed. "Why ever would you say such a thing?" The color began to rise in her cheeks. "Nobody is *here* against their will or chained up at night."

"Oh, I know that," Moira said, flushing with embarrassment. "I just meant to say that you are purveyors of flesh the same as them."

"We are *not* the same as them," Mattie snapped and set her cup and saucer onto the side table with a resounding clink of the delicate china. "The women working here get paid for everything they do and the House just takes a percentage. In return, they get a nice room in a nice house, good food anytime they want it, and a nice wardrobe." Mattie gestured around the ornate parlor. "You certainly can't compare *this* to being chained up in a cat wagon, servicing men on pallets out on the cold ground."

"Oh, to be sure," Moira said and sipped daintily from the porcelain cup. "And I meant no offence. I was just surprised. At first I took ye for fine ladies from the church or something not ..." Her voice trailed off in embarrassment.

"Not whores?" Roxie said with a grin on her face and amusement in her tone. "I'm beggin your pardon, lass," she said, aping Moira's Irish accent, "but I think I'd rather be called a whore than a fine lady from the church."

"I'll second that," Mattie said lifting her cup in salute, "any day."

"You don't get on with the church then?" Moira asked wide-eyed. "I don't suppose I do now either, but you shouldn't blaspheme ..." Moira swallowed hard and lifted her eyes as if trying to see whether or not God was looking down on their discussion. "Tis a sin."

"Sugar," Roxie said with a soft smile, "I'm thirty-four years old and figure I've got a few more good years left in me. I'm gonna enjoy them and then find a good father to hear my confession, say a few Hail Maries in contrition and be absolved. If that's the way you were raised, then I suggest you do the same and quit frettin' over things you can't change."

Mattie watched the girl biting the inside of her mouth. "Moira, nobody is forcing you to stay here. You are free to leave at any time."

The girl's brilliant green eyes darted between the two women. "You don't want me to ... eh ... to do anything to pay you back for everything you've done for me—de food, de room, and de fine clothes?" Her long delicate fingers brushed over the soft cotton skirt she wore, settling to finger the lace edging the decorative apron.

"Absolutely not," Roxie said as she bent and poured more tea into their cups. "You're free to go and do as you please. You're welcome to stay here as long as you'd like or you can go back home to Chicago. We'll not try and stop you and we'll even buy your ticket."

"I'll not be goin' back to Chicago," she said softly, but firmly with a shake of her head that flipped her auburn curls over her shoulders. "Do you think Harley and Pete are still out there lookin' for me?"

"It's been three weeks, Sugar," Roxie sighed. "Has he ever searched for anybody that long or stayed in one place just to look for one runaway girl?"

She shook her head, "No, and I heard dem sayin' dey wanted t' be headin' back t' Colorado t' de gold fields an' leave us off wid some men dere before headin' back east for fresh stock." That last came out as a sour sneer. "Dey didn't even dink of us as any better dan cattle or sheep."

"Men like them should be shot," Roxie spat "but I don't think you have to worry about them anymore. They've probably made their way out of the Territory and back into Colorado by now."

Roxie knew exactly the sort of place awaited the girls in that wagon. Marty Rowe had threatened to take Roxie to one where she'd be kept in a cage like an animal and used by filthy miners for the nickel or dime the cage owners could collect for the poke. They'd be fed on scraps and cock juice until they starved or froze to death in the Rocky Mountain cold.

"You're safe here, Sugar," Roxie assured the auburn-haired girl, "until you decide what you want to do."

"I appreciate it. I really do. I don't know what would o' become o' me had ye not found me by de road dat day."

"You're a good girl, Moira," Roxie sighed. "I'm so sorry this had to happen to you the way it did. As women, sometimes our innocence is stolen away from us before our virtue and that's a shame. We should be allowed to give up our virtues of our own accords while we're still innocent and still believe in the fantasy of love and living happily-ever-after with the man of our dreams."

***

Ten days later as all the women of the Victoriana sat in the parlor reading and discussing the events in the day's newspaper over late-morning coffee, somebody pounded on the front door with the big brass lion-head knocker. Too early for Jessie to be on duty, Mattie rose and went to the door. She cracked it open to see two men in shabby clothes and dusty, scuffed boots standing on the porch.

"I'm sorry gentlemen," she said politely, "but we won't be open for business until five this evening. If you'd care to …" The bigger man pushed open the door knocking Mattie aside easily.

"I don't care to do shit, whore," he growled as he stomped past her into the foyer. "I was told down in town that you have some property of mine and I want it back."

A taller lanky man who smelled strongly of body odor followed him in staring around the big open foyer with its ornate chandelier and wide stairway leading upward with its polished banister. "Not bad," he said and whistled. "You must get a pretty penny for your cunny to pay for a fancy place like this." To his partner he said, "Harley, I bet they've got a good bit of coin stashed around here. We should relieve 'em of it while we're collectin' the cunt."

Mattie suddenly realized who stood in her foyer and her mind began to race. "I have no idea what you're talking about, sir, now kindly leave my house," she demanded loudly, following Harley as he walked slowly toward the parlor where Moira sat, unsuspecting, with the others. She grabbed him by the shoulder and tried to stop him. He rounded on Mattie and slapped her hard. She went to the floor with the force of the blow and she heard Pete laughing behind her.

"Keep your filthy hands off me, whore," Harley growled, glaring down at her. He kicked Mattie hard in the ribs, taking her breath away momentarily. "I think I'll give you a good ass-fucking to teach you some manners and that your actions have consequences." Harley grabbed a hand full of red curls and yanked Mattie to her feet. "I came into town here to collect my wayward property. The man at the telegraph office said he'd seen the two of you with it in your buggy back about the time it went missin'," Harley sneered. "I was all polite-like, but you're a whore and had to go gettin' mouthy with me." He yanked her hair again, and Mattie let out a loud yelp of pain.

"Get your damned filthy hands off me, you scum," Mattie yelped as he tugged harder on her hair.

Her yelp brought the women from the parlor rushing into the foyer.

"Oh dear Jesus, Mary, and Joseph," Moira wailed and pushed past the staring women to run for the stairs.

"Was that her, Harley?" Pete asked his partner as he watched Moira's behind rush up the stairs. "She looks a might different in fancy bedclothes and with her hair all combed up. She might even bring two dollars a poke now."

"She ain't gonna be nothin' but coyote bait after I'm done with her," Harley growled and moved to follow Moira up the stairs. "She knowed the consequences of runnin' for a third time."

Pete whistled as he stared at the women gathered in the foyer helping Mattie to her feet and making a barrier between Harley and the fleeing Moira. "Will you look at all this high-dollar cunny, Harley," he called to his scowling partner. He reached a dirty hand out to grab one of the girls' behind through her thin dressing gown. "Come here, darlin' I wanna see if high-dollar cunny feels any different than the cunny of those cat wagon tramps out there." He jerked his head toward the wagon parked in the front drive.

"You're a disgusting piece of filth," hissed Martha, shaking her brunette curls as she turned to dislodge his hand from her behind. "I'll thank you to keep your dirty hands off me."

"You hear that Harley," he sneered and grabbed Martha's breast, twisting it savagely, "this mouthy little cunt wants me to keep my hands *off* her. I guess she thinks she's too good for a simple working man after fucking men with money in this place. I think we should strip her and drag her out to the wagon and give her some lessons on how to treat a real man." He drew back and punched Martha in the face, sending her flying into the arms of the other women while he laughed hysterically at the sight of female bodies tumbling down in a mass of curls, lace, and satin ribbons. "We could just walk in here and take over. All this cunny could be ours to sell to the highest bidder."

"Miss Mattie done asked you to be leavin' sir," said a voice from behind Pete, but before he could turn to see who addressed him, a heavy vase came crashing down upon his balding head and he crumpled to the floor with blood beginning to seep from his dirty ears.

Harley had turned to answer his scrawny partner, but turned back toward the stairs after he saw Pete go down. When he turned a petite blonde in a blue dressing gown blocked his path to the stairs.

"Get out of my way, bitch or I'll give you some of what I intend to give the redhead over there after I collect my property." He squeezed his crotch as if to threaten Roxie.

"Sugar," she sneered sweetly in her heaviest southern drawl, "unless you're packin' a Gatlin' gun in them drawers I ain't much worried."

"I just came to collect my wayward property," he howled. He reached into his pocket and drew out a bundle of folded papers. "That girl belongs to me. I got me a legal paper signed by her daddy back in Chicago, givin' me rights to her until the time I see her legally wed. Until that time, she's mine to do with as I see fit."

"I have good reason to know slavery was outlawed in this country some years ago," Roxie snarled as she grabbed the papers from his dirty hand.

"She's no slave, but that paper makes me her legal guardian. Her daddy signed it. She's mine to control until she's wed or dead," he sneered. "I had it drawn up by an attorney in Chicago and it's all legal-like. That girl is *mine*." He took another step forward.

"You told those girls' parents you were going to find them husbands, but you've just been takin' them across the territories pimping them out in mining camps and at military posts. How do you figure that's finding them husbands?" Roxie tossed the stack of papers back at him.

Harley laughed from deep in his barrel chest. "How do you think? No man buys a horse without giving it a good test-ride first. I just take the girls to places where there are men who want to give them a good ride to test 'em out and who are willing to pay for it," he said with tears running from his eyes as he laughed. "I ain't got no fancy house," Harley said, gesturing around the room, "but you're no better than me, bitch. I offer cunts for sale and *you* offer cunts for sale."

"That's true, but my girls knew exactly what they were getting into when they signed on with me. I didn't lie to them and I don't keep them chained up and starved half to death," Roxie snarled. "You're a lying, thieving, contemptuous piece of shit." Roxie looked up at the women standing around the unmoving man on the floor. "One of you girls run get the constable. We've got a kidnapper, a slave trader, and a murderer here to be arrested."

"Damnit, whore, I wanted to have a little fun before giving that little cunt her punishment." He cleared his throat loudly and spat the phlegm onto the floor at Roxie's feet. "I'd really like to teach you a little lesson too," he snarled at Roxie. "You need to learn the *consequences* of crossing a real man," he said and squeezed his bulging crotch again.

"As I said before, Sugar," Roxie said, rolling her big blue eyes and grinning at the scowling pimp, "You ain't got nothin' in them drawers that would scare me—no matter where you wanted to put it." She glared at him with contempt. "And Moira said that little cock of yours wouldn't even stretch out a cat's cunny. You're no kind of *man* at all. You're not even the scab off a *real* man's ass."

Harley's face grew dark and he drew his hand back to deliver a hard blow, but his narrowed eyes went wide as Roxie lifted and pointed her little double-barreled Derringer at his fat belly. She pulled both triggers to deliver a shot that opened Harley's bowels to spill out onto the parquet tiles in a wreaking, bloody mess. He let out a surprised yelp of pain and dismay before falling backward with his eyes rolling back into his head as he took one last gasping breath of his own putrid stench.

Roxie glanced over to see Mary and Elsie standing with Minnie over the sprawled body of Pete in the foyer. "I'm ever so sorry about this god-awful mess, ladies. I suppose we can put off openin' tonight until six so we can get it cleaned up." She bent over and took a set of iron keys from Harley's belt. She tossed them to Mattie. "Go let those poor things out of that wagon and bring them in here for some food and hot bathes."

Virgil Earp and two other constables arrived to take everyone's statements and pronounced the shooting death of Harley Duncan a case of obvious self-defense. Peter Lewis wasn't dead and they hauled him off unceremoniously to the jail where Doc Robinson tended his fractured

132 |Lori Beasley Bradley

skull. He was indicted on charges of kidnapping, rape, and pandering, but to everyone's amazement, only sentenced to six months in the Territorial prison in Yuma.

"I don't know what to say, Roxie," Virgil said, shaking his head, as the courtroom emptied, "that curly wolf should have hanged for treatin' those girls like that. If it weren't for that cracked skull Miss Minnie gave him, he'd be swingin' tomorrow. As it is, he'll probably do easy time in the prison infirmary and probably won't even do the whole six months."

"I could always have the girls waitin' for him along the trail to Yuma," Roxie said with a giggle. "I bet they'd make short work of his scrawny hide if they got their hands on him."

Virgil raised one thick black eyebrow. "I certainly wouldn't want to be wearin' his drawers if they did." He chuckled.

The women from the wagon had been carried into the Victoriana where they were fed, bathed, and restored to some semblance of health by Mattie and Miss Minnie. Three, including Moira, decided to stay on at the Victoriana, three others took the stage east to return to Chicago, and the remaining three took rooms elsewhere in town, hoping to find husbands amongst the miners and ranch hands who frequented Prescott.

Chapter 15

September 15, 1879

Loud voices at the door grabbed Roxie's attention as she sat in the parlor, enjoying a glass of Tennessee whiskey with some of the women as they waited for clients and she rose to investigate. As a rule, the men visiting the Victoriana were a refined and quiet bunch. They received few men who hadn't already heard about the high prices expected for an hour with a woman at the Victoriana and few rowdy cowboys, drunken miners, or loud gamblers graced their doorway.

"We want us that little yellow-haired whore we talked to on the Fourth," bellowed the man at the door. "Come on out here, we want our free pokes."

Roxie rolled her eyes as she recognized the voice of John Dewey, the owner of the big Dewey Ranch east of Prescott and wondered why it had taken him so long to collect the poke she'd promised two months before on the night of the grand opening party.

"Mr. Dewey," Roxie said with an animated sweet smile on her pretty face, "how very nice to see you again." She turned to his smaller but sharper dressed companion. "And Mr. Ramsay, how good of you to come." She reached out her tiny hand for his. "Why don't you come into the parlor and you can have the pick of the available girls waitin' there."

Dewey took a long stride forward and hooked an arm around Roxie's slender waist.

"Now hold on just a minute, sweetheart," he said and gazed down into Roxie's blue eyes. "We're here to have a taste of *your* sweet cunny, not the hired help's." He reached into his pocket and pulled out the business cards Roxie had given him. "You want both of these if we only want the *one* girl?" He asked with a wicked grin creasing his ruddy face.

Roxie tugged both cards from John Dewey's beefy fingers and frowned at his dirty fingernails. "Do you *both* plan to use her?"

"Well, of course we do," Dewey said with a chuckle from deep in his broad chest.

"Then, yes," Roxie said, tucking the cards into the pocket of her dressing gown. "If you both plan to play, then you both have to pay."

"Typical whore," Dewey huffed before taking her petite hand into his large one. "Well, lead the way so we can drain our ballocks out into ya."

"Is everything alright, Miss Roxie?" Martha asked, coming out of the parlor with a crystal glass of whiskey in her hand.

"It's fine, Martha," Roxie said, but took the glass of whiskey from her hand and sipped. "I'm just taking these fine gents up to my room for an hour's pleasure."

"Yes, ma'am," Martha said, giving Roxie and both men a narrow-eyed glare.

She probably thinks I'm taking business away from her and the opportunity for a good tip. Mattie and I seldom take clients. I wish Martha knew how much I really don't want to be soiling my bed linens with these two rascals.

Roxie led the two men across the foyer and up the wide stairs. They crossed the ballroom and down the hall where the other girls had their rooms until they came to the narrow stairs that led up to her and Mattie's attic rooms.

"Damnit woman," Dewey huffed as he began to climb the second set of stairs. "You better be worth it. I ain't never had to climb so many damned stairs to climb up on a whore before. Have you, Al?"

"No," Ramsay said, panting as he latched a hand playfully onto Roxie's behind, "but I'm betting this little cunny's worth every damned step."

"Just what do you boys have in mind?" Roxie asked as her foot stepped onto the landing and twisted her way out of Ramsay's grasp.

"You have a big mirror in that bedroom of yours?" Dewey asked.

"Of course," Roxie said as she sashayed ahead of the men, the silk of her dressing gown and petticoat swishing around her legs.

"Al here likes to watch a gal suck my cock while he sticks his in her from behind," Dewey explained. "I bet that pretty little mouth is gonna feel really good around it, too," he said as Roxie opened the door to her room and led the red-faced men inside.

Roxie eyed the big man. His crudeness surprised her somewhat. Though a cattle rancher, he mixed in what passed for Prescott's high society with other business owners, politicians, and their wives. Such might be tolerated amongst wranglers on a ranch, but not in even this rough-and-tumble town's elite company.

As much as I'd like to think, I suppose Red and I are still just low class dirty whores in the minds of some people and always will be no matter how elegant our house is or how much we charge for our services.

The Victoriana boasted two turrets on the street-side of the third floor with stained glass windows and those rooms housed Roxie and Mattie's furnishings. The carpenters had managed to install two privy closets in the slant-roofed area between the turrets so both women could attend to their necessaries in private.

At the foot of Roxie's bed set a cedar chest with a cushioned top and she took a seat upon it while the men stared around the Wedgewood blue room with its silver embossed tin ceiling tiles and bright-white moldings. The stained glass window cast a rainbow of colors across the polished pine floor and white satin coverlet on her bed.

"Will these mirrors in the wardrobe do?" Roxie asked nodding at the oval mirrors set into the doors of the tall free-standing pine closet.

"They certainly will," Ramsay said and yanked Roxie around to try and plant a sloppy, wet kiss upon her mouth.

Roxie turned her face away, avoiding his mustached mouth. "You'd best get your drawers off, Sugar You only have an hour," she said matter-of-factly.

"Yah," Dewey sneered, "well you better get your clothes off, too, sweetheart. We like to have our whores completely naked." He slipped the leather vest off his shoulders and tossed it over the chair at the vanity. Roxie watched him begin unbuttoning his sturdy brown trousers. Though Dewey had put on a clean shirt and string tie for their visit to the Victoriana, his trousers were dusty and sweat-stained from a day's work on his ranch.

Ramsay had already taken off and carefully folded his black silk jacket and white, starched shirt. Thick gray hair covered his broad chest. Pasty skin stretched tight over his broad shoulders and muscular upper arms that seldom saw the sun. Roxie thought both men to be in their early to mid-fifties. While Dewey's body was tanned from many hours in the sun, shirtless, Ramsay's, while fit, was pallid, giving the appearance of softness. She ran a hand over his shoulders and they were not soft in the least. This man knew hard work as well as Dewey did.

He turned back to Roxie and pulled gently on the satin tie that held her dressing gown closed. He pushed it off her pale, smooth shoulders and it fell to puddle upon the floor around her petite bare feet. He undid the tiny buttons of her camisole and nudged it open to reveal her small, firm bosoms. Ramsay pushed off the camisole and it joined the dressing gown at her feet before pulling at the tie securing her petticoat. He loosened it and slid it down past her narrow hips and firm, round ass cheeks.

Ramsay took Roxie's nipples between his thumbs and forefingers, pinching and twisting until she gasped with the pain. It would have been a pleasurable pain had this not been a business transaction, but it was, and Roxie bit her tongue and allowed him to continue, ignoring the throbbing between her thighs. She didn't generally allow herself to be excited by the attentions of customer, but Alan Ramsay *did* excite her and Roxie didn't know what to think about that.

"Crawl up on the bed and get on your hands and knees," he directed, gazing at their reflections in the big oval mirrors with a look of anticipation on his handsome angular face. Though tanned from riding to his mining operations, his cheeks were sunken. His thin lips were drawn up into a leering smile as he stared at their reflections in the mirror. Brown eyes rimmed with thick dark lashes under heavy brows sparkled with his smile as he gazed back at Roxie.

Roxie rolled her eyes and obeyed reluctantly. Ramsay took off his trousers and folded them to place with his jacket and shirt. Roxie noted with a private smile that this man, at least, had taken the time to clean up and dress nicely for his visit. He then joined Roxie on the bed, crawling up behind her and massaging the cheeks of her naked ass. A finger slid into her cunny and she heard him give a soft sigh of approval. She involuntarily tightened her cunny around his finger in response to the unexpected throbbing there.

"Nice tight little cunny and wet too," he sighed as he eased his finger in and out of her.

Dewey's big body rocked the bed as he joined them, threatening to toss them off the swaying mattress as he positioned himself on his knees in front of Roxie. His big, rough hand held his hard cock, stroking it gently. He grabbed Roxie's blonde hair and yanked her head down toward his groin. She smelled bay rum wafting up from the course black tuft of hair fringing his stiff cock and dangling ballocks.

Roxie saw him staring into the mirror. "Suck on this," he said roughly and pressed Roxie's head down until her lips parted and she took the stiff organ into her mouth. It wasn't very long or thick and she could take the entire cock without gagging. "Ahhh," he groaned with pleasure as she tightened her lips around him. He began rocking his hips to force his penis in and out. "You in yet, Al?" Dewey gasped. "I ain't had none in a while, so this ain't gonna take me long." His hips moved faster and he pulled Roxie's hair.

Why do they always have to pull the damned hair?

Ramsay's warm fingers spread her ass cheeks and his hard cock jammed into Roxie's waiting cunny. Fingers dug into the tender flesh as he began to pound into her from behind. It took Roxie a few minutes to synchronize the rhythm between Ramsay's thrusts from behind and Dewey's in her face, but soon she had it and rocked on her knees with the movement of both men's sweating bodies.

"Here it comes, Al," Dewey moaned, "You want to see it all over her pretty painted face?"

"Oh, yah," Ramsay panted, "and in her hair too."

Damnit! Now I'm gonna have to wash it before I go to bed. I hate goin' to bed with wet hair.

"Alright," Dewey roared and yanked his erection from Roxie's mouth and stroked it frantically with his big fist. He grunted loudly and hot liquid shot onto Roxie's flushed face and up into her disheveled, blonde hair. "Damn she sucks cock nice," Dewey panted and slumped back against the headboard as his erection wilted into the course black hair of his sweaty groin. Dewey twisted Roxie's head so Ramsay could see the thick white fluid running down her cheeks and into her eyes from what he'd deposited into her hair.

"Want me to turn her around so she can swallow yours, too?" Dewey offered with a grin.

"No," Ramsay grunted, "I'm gonna deposit mine somewhere else." He pulled his wet cock out of Roxie's cunny and she groaned mentally as she felt him maneuvering it up to slam into the puckered orifice between her open ass cheeks. She grunted with the sudden pain of being taken there without the benefit of perfumed lard for lubrication and Dewey began to laugh at her obvious discomfort.

"Give it to that little asshole good, Al. I think she likes it."

Refusing to go away from this encounter frustrated, Roxie eased her hand up between her thighs and began massaging the throbbing bud there. As her pleasure began to take her, Roxie met Ramsay thrust for thrust until her body tensed and her groin exploded in waves of exquisite delight. She suppressed a gasp, but the men were ignoring her, engrossed in their own amusement.

"I am, buddy," Ramsay groaned, "I am." Roxie felt his speed increase and his hands gripped her ass cheeks tighter. She grimaced, knowing she'd have purple bruises in the morning from his fingers. "Oh, Jesus," he yelled as he shoved deep into her with his release. "Oh, shit," he panted and went limp over her bent back. His heart pounded against hers as he breathed heavily into her ear and stared into the big oval mirrors. "We are definitely going to do this again," he whispered and winked at her reflection. "You are one fine bit of cunny."

Roxie waited until his pounding heart slowed to a normal rhythm before sitting up and rolling Ramsay from her back. She didn't want a repeat of what had happened with Garrison in the stage to Cimarron. "I hope you gents enjoyed yourselves. If you're thinkin' on doin' this again," she said, throwing her legs over the bed, sliding into her slippers, and walking to the wash stand, "it will cost you twenty dollars," she paused for effect, "*each.*"

"Damn," Dewey said, losing his grin and staring wide-eyed at Ramsay, "the whore thinks a lot of her goods."

"Yes, I do," Roxie said, wetting a cloth to wipe Dewey's deposit from her face and hair with a narrow-eyed frown.

I'm gonna start quotin' an extra dollar for messin' up my damned hair.

"I can buy a prize bull for less than twenty dollars," Dewey spat as he reached for his trousers crumpled on the floor.

"Good, then get *him* to suck your cock next time." Roxie rinsed the cloth and whipped her tender behind, catching Ramsay's deposit as it began to seep out of her anus.

Ramsay began to laugh. "She's got ya there, John and I don't think I'd want to go stickin' my Johnson into any of your damned bulls." He buttoned his trousers and then reached into his pocket. He came out with a twenty-dollar gold piece between his fingers and dropped it onto Roxie's vanity. "Thank you, Miss Roxie, for a very enjoyable afternoon."

Roxie eyed Ramsay and then the gold coin before smiling sweetly. "Why thank you kindly, sir, any time." They both glanced at Dewey who had finished tying his string-tie and was slipping back into his vest.

"I don't know what you're glaring at me for," he snarled. "I came here for a *free* poke. I hope you're not expecting to be paid now that it's all done and over with." He sat on the edge of the bed and pulled on his dusty boots.

"Not at all," Roxie said and picked up one of the business cards they'd presented to her earlier. She handed it to Ramsay. "*You* sir are welcome to come see me again." She picked up her clothes from the floor and walked toward the privy closet. "I'm sure you can find your way back down to the parlor." Roxie went inside and closed the door.

"What the hell did she mean by that?" Roxie heard Dewey say.

"You're an idiot, John," Ramsay said before the door to Roxie's room closed and she heard their boots clacking against the wooden floor of the hall as they walked toward the stairs.

Roxie grinned to herself and ran a brush through her hair. She dabbed a bit of lavender oil behind her ears and then got back into her clothes. She stared at her face in the mirror. She bent closer to the mirror noting tiny lines at the corners of her eyes.

I swear those weren't there a month ago. Willard always said management put extra years on a soul. Maybe he was right after all. I'd never have fathomed managing a whorehouse would be so much bother. Mattie tends to the paperwork and ordering of the liquor, but dealin with employees is like herdin' cats, especially female employees. This one thinks the other one got a prettier dress, or is gettin' clients who tip better, while the other one complains about the hours or the number of clients. They have my head all caddywampus and now I'm getting' wrinkles to boot.

She heard a tap at her door and sighed. She rolled her eyes, tightened the satin bow on her dressing gown, and went to the door. She opened it to find Mattie standing there with a crystal glass filled with Tennessee whiskey in one hand.

"I thought you might need this," her redheaded friend said with a sheepish grin.

Roxie eagerly took the glass from her friend. "You're a mind reader, Red, and a life saver."

Mattie took her hand from the pocket of her dressing gown and stuck it out. "Here, the big fella said to give you this." Roxie stretched out her empty hand and Mattie dropped two ten-dollar gold pieces into her palm. "What the hell was goin' on up here?"

Roxie shrugged her shoulders and gave her friend a blank look. "Nothin' out of the ordinary."

"Uhuh," Mattie said and held the door as Roxie walked out into the hall, sipping her whiskey and grinning broadly.

Chapter 16

October 16, 1879

Mattie strolled casually along the boardwalk up Whiskey Row, humming a happy tune, on her way to Riley's Mercantile, where she planned to place a very large order for fabrics. She and Roxie had decided the women should have new dressing gowns for the winter season made of velvet in the shades their rooms were painted, as well as new gowns for the holiday parties they intended to host at the Victoriana for the less fortunate of Prescott and the surrounding area.

A cholera outbreak during the summer in some of the mining camps to the south had brought an influx of orphaned children into town, as well as, several penniless widows with hungry children to feed. The churches were having difficulties providing and she and Roxie had decided to follow their mentor from St. Louis, Madam Ophelia's lead and host galas for both Thanksgiving and Christmas.

"Hello, Mrs. Kirby," Mrs. Riley said from behind the counter after the bell above the door rang announcing Mattie's entrance into the dry goods store. "What can I do for *you* today?"

"Mr. Riley gave me some fabric samples last week and I want to place the order so Mrs. Clayton to get to work on the projects." Mattie said cheerfully as she wiped her muddy boots on the mat before stepping onto the polished wood floor of the store that smelled of coal oil, candle wax, and dust. She held the bundle of fabric swatches in her gloved hand.

"I wondered what had happened to those," the middle-aged woman, wearing her mousy-brown hair in a severe bun and with wire-rimmed spectacles stretched across her aquiline nose said in a sour tone as she glared at Mattie, whose mood dampened with the woman's disapproving frown. "I had customers waiting for them to get here from St. Louis so *they* could place orders for their children's winter clothes."

"I'm so sorry, but I wanted to take them home so Roxie could help me choose the colors and Mr. Riley didn't tell me there was any rush to get them back. I thought it would be easier doing the choosing there than dragging Roxie down here to argue it through in the middle of your store." Mattie smiled and started to add what garments the fabrics would be made into, but Mrs. Riley's intense scowl caused her to hold her tongue.

Though they had spent hundreds of dollars at Riley's Mercantile, furnishing and outfitting the Victoriana and Mr. Riley had always been accommodating and appreciative of their business, Mrs. Riley seemed to be less so. "Of course, you did," the woman sneered and reached for the bundle of fabric samples.

"Have I done something to offend you, ma'am?" Mattie asked, surprised and irritated by Mrs. Riley's irksome demeanor.

"I'm a good Christian woman, madam," she said with her eyes narrowed in contempt. "Your filthy, flesh-peddling business and your very presence in my good store offends me," she snapped and her voice echoed in the cavernous store, empty except for the two of them. Mattie began to understand the absence of bodies in the store if the woman was this rude to all her paying customers.

"I see," Mattie said and let the bundle of swatches slip from her gloved fingers. A door closed on the floor above and Mattie heard boots start down the stairs. "I'll be going then and will take my offensive business over to Crider's where they're a bit more tolerant of me and my business."

"Crider is a green-grocer," Mrs. Riley said smugly with a chuckle as her husband walked up to the counter, gazing open-mouthed between the two glowering women. "He can't possibly accommodate your needs for fabrics and *other* goods."

"On the contrary," Mattie said firmly and loudly, "Mr. Crider has assured me *many* times over the past several months that he can supply us at the Victoriana with anything we might need above and beyond groceries. He carries general merchandise as well, and has promised me competitive prices for the same goods I've been purchasing regularly here." Mattie met Mr. Riley's eyes that had gone wide, his mind, no doubt tallying the losses it would cost his mercantile should she walk out of his store and across the street to Crider's. Mattie glared back at Mrs. Riley. "Neither he nor Mrs. Crider find me and my business offensive, so I'll gladly take it there."

Mattie turned toward the door and Mr. Riley touched her shoulder gently to halt her progress. "What's going on here, Mrs. Kirby? What's all this about getting your dry goods at Crider's?"

"Ask your wife," Mattie snapped and yanked her shoulder from his grasp. "I'll be on my way now, so me and my ill-gotten coin don't offend this good Christian lady any longer."

"What?" he gulped and glared fleetingly at his wife who stood behind the counter with a haughty, self-satisfied look on her face. "I'm sure my wife meant no offence …"

"On the contrary, Mr. Riley," Mattie continued firmly. "I'm the one your wife finds offensive and I'd rather do my business with a merchant who *isn't* offended by my presence or my money in her store." She glowered at Mrs. Riley again. "I wish you'd told me how offended you were by my business before I spent all that money here last summer." She returned her eyes to Mr. Riley, whose face had drained of its color. "I'll remedy that now, though, and take the business of the Victoriana to the Criders or up to stores in Flagstaff."

"We don't need the filthy money earned by this whoring filth," Mrs. Riley said to her scowling husband, though weakly.

"Will you shut your goddamned mouth, woman," Mattie heard Mr. Riley yell as she stepped out onto the board walk.

"God will reward us for our courage," Mrs. Riley retorted.

"You have no idea what you've done, you stupid old fool," Riley admonished. "That woman's business was the only thing *keeping* us in business. Before those women began buying from us, we were on the verge of bankruptcy. Crider was about to put *us* out of business, but now *you've* gone and done it with your fool mouth."

Mattie stopped abruptly when she heard the sound of a hard slap being delivered. She very nearly turned to go back in, but heard Mrs. Riley's weeping reply.

"If the damned whore wants to shop at Crider's, then so be it. God will reward us for turning away their sinful business, Robert. You'll see."

"You're a goddamned idiot, woman. Why don't you move your belongings down to that fool church and let *them* feed and clothe you for a while."

Mattie stepped down off the boardwalk and crossed the muddy street, walking toward Crider's Grocery and General Merchandise, mentally putting together an order that would set the Riley's teeth on edge and their cheeks green with envy. Not one to be vindictive by nature, Mattie surprised herself by wondering how she could spread the total of the order she planned to place with the Criders now and how to be there to see the Riley's faces when they heard about it.

I'll never understand how some people will go out of their way to cut off their noses just to spite their faces. Rox and I have spent hundreds of dollars over the past year getting the Victoriana set up and hundreds more with their friends they recommended. Hell, that bitch's brother was one of the finish carpenters we hired along with his nephew who did the painting.

I think she really thought I'd still have to buy from Riley's because there was no other place in town. Serves her right for being ignorant of her own business. Self-righteous bitch.

After placing an order with Mrs. Crider, using her personal fabric swatches, for twice the fabric she'd planned to order, choosing a new set of china with tea and coffee services, and silver vanity sets for all the girls, including Miss Minnie and her girls, Mattie marched home to explain her expenditures to Roxie.

"I never liked that sour, old bitch," Roxie grumbled as she poured Mattie a double shot of Tennessee whiskey from the crystal decanter in the parlor. "If I'd been there, I'd have slapped her silly."

"If you'd been there," Mattie said, relieved Roxie didn't mind her extravagant, angry shopping spree at Crider's, "you'd probably have taken out your gun, challenged her to a dual, and shot her between her beady, little eyes."

Roxie burst out laughing. "Duals are matters of honor. That bitch has none. I'd have just shot her."

"Humph," Mattie agreed, "but how would we have bailed you out of jail?"

"With the money you spent on china and vanity sets."

Mattie tipped up her glass and drained the whiskey in one long swallow. "Don't be angry, Rox. I thought we could give them as Christmas presents. They're nice sets with a boar's bristle hair brush, a comb, and hand mirror on a little silver tray with two pretty little scent bottles."

"They sound nice," Roxie said with a grin, "and I won't be angry if you got one for me, too."

Chapter 17

November 20, 1879

"I can't believe this bullshit," Roxie stormed and pitched the folded sheet of paper and envelope at Mattie.

"What is it?" Mattie asked as she picked up the paper from the floor where it had landed.

"We've been *invited* to a meeting of the Whiskey Row Improvement League."

"Whiskey Row Improvement League, what the hell is that? I've never heard of it," Mattie said reading over the piece of creamy stationary. "Is it some temperance league trying to clean up the town?"

"Hardly," Roxie sputtered and furrowed her brow, "That's Jim Hardy's signature at the bottom."

Mattie scanned the letter again, her face draining of color, studying the flamboyant signature of James F. Hardy at the bottom. "But Hardy owns the Peacock Saloon on Whiskey Row …"

"And runs half the girls in the cribs down there, too. He's by far the most dangerous man in Prescott." Roxie poured two glasses of whiskey and handed one to Mattie. "We must be eating into his business somehow," Roxie said and tipped up her glass to take a long swallow. "This can't be good."

"Are we gonna go?" Mattie asked nervously.

"I don't see how we can avoid it," Roxie sputtered and threw her hands into the air. "You don't just go ignoring written invitations from Jim Hardy."

Mattie peered at the neatly penned letter. "It says here he wants to meet on Sunday at three o'clock in the salon at the Palace Hotel. That's a pretty public place." She sipped her drink, but her hands had begun to tremble with Roxie's apparent unease about the summons to this meeting. "Surely he wouldn't be planning anything dangerous if he's inviting us to the Palace when the Sunday luncheon crowd is bound to be there."

Roxie took another long swallow, draining her glass. "That's a good point," Roxie said and Mattie thought her little friend looked somewhat relieved. "I just can't imagine what this is all about."

"It's probably nothing to worry about, Rox." Mattie tried to sound positive, but she'd heard stories about Jim Hardy's temper and brutal methods. She took hold of her glass with her other hand to stop it from shaking. "How are things coming with the preparations for our big Thanksgiving dinner?" Perhaps changing the subject would lighten Roxie's somber mood.

Roxie rolled her eyes and grinned weakly. "Poor Elsie has been runnin' non-stop back and forth to Crider's for this thing and that. They're startin' on the bread and the pies today."

"But it's only Monday."

"Yes," Roxie said with a raised eyebrow, "But they're cookin' for a hundred ... and you know how folks eat when the food's free."

"That I do," Mattie said and rolled her eyes, remembering the grand opening party. "What's on the menu?

"Why turkey birds, of course," said Miss Minnie shuffling into the parlor wearing a blue calico dress, white apron, and blue head cloth to match her dress. "And we'll have nice fat hams, sweet potatoes, mashed white potatoes, stuffing from the birds, collard greens, and gravy made from the meat drippin's from the birds and the hams. Do that sound like enough?" She asked with a nervous grin.

"That sounds wonderful, Minnie, just wonderful," Mattie said, giving the tiny Negro woman an awkward stare. "Did you need something, Minnie?" The old cook seldom ventured out of her kitchen and Mattie suspected something important troubled her.

"This is goin' to be such a big party upstairs, I was just wonderin' if you really want to mess with mixin' in all my folks, as well. I wouldn't want there to be no trouble on that account."

Race relations in Prescott were not good, but Roxie and Mattie wanted to open the Victoriana to everyone in need. They'd asked Miss Minnie to invite some of the needy from her community, but the woman had been reluctant.

"I just don't think it's a good idea to be seatin' black folk with white."

"I swear Minnie," Roxie insisted, "If any of those tight-ass whites give your people any shit, I'll …"

"It's not your folks I'm concerned over," Minnie said hesitantly. "It's mine. Some don't cotton to eatin' at the same table with white trash."

Mattie slapped a hand to her mouth to keep from laughing and Roxie's face paled.

"Oh my gracious, Minnie," she said, trying to keep a straight face, but thinking quick about the situation. "Rox, are we going to be using the private dining room downstairs? If Miss Minnie would be more comfortable with it, we could set up tables in there and she and her folks could enjoy their Thanksgiving in there."

"That would be a better idea, Miss Roxie," Minnie let out a long breath and said with a smile creasing her leathery brown face. "Some of the menfolk likes to partake of a little shine with their dinner and the white folks might not appreciate our particular brand of merriment."

"Of course," Roxie said relieved, "Y'all can set up in the private theatre and enjoy your own dinner and entertainments while the white folk eat upstairs and enjoy *our* entertainments." Roxie had arranged for the same orchestra that had played for them at the grand opening party and she knew the Negros probably wouldn't enjoy it as much as they would their own musicians.

"I'm so sorry, Minnie. I should have thought this through a little better," Roxie apologized, taking Minnie's brown hand into hers and kissing them warmly. "I just wanted you and yours to feel included here."

"Me and my girls know that Miss Roxie and we appreciate you both so much for the thought. We know how things are between black and white folks, though, and wouldn't want to cause you no trouble over it."

"Of course you wouldn't," Roxie sighed as she watched the cook shuffle off back to the kitchen where the scent of pies baking filled the house.

The Thanksgiving festivities went off without a hitch. Tables for thirty were set up in the private dining room off the kitchen for the Negros invited, while a little more than a hundred men, women, and children filled the trestle tables and benches set up in the ballroom upstairs.

Miss Minnie and her girls outdid themselves with the succulent turkeys and smoky hams, creamy potatoes, and tasty baked goods. At the end of the day, most of the trays and bowls had been scraped clean with bony carcasses piled high to be tossed out to the hungry dogs that roamed the streets of the growing town.

"What a wonderful day," Roxie said to Mattie as they sat together in the empty and blessedly quiet kitchen over pumpkin pie with thick, sweetened whipped cream and hot coffee. "Don't you think Madam Ophelia would have been impressed, Red?"

"Yes, I think she'd be right proud of you, Rox."

"She'd be proud of the both of us, Red. We've come a long way in the past nine years. You were just a down and out Kentucky Cracker and I was a used up crib girl. Now we own the nicest House in the Arizona Territory … and probably the entire lands west of the Mississippi. Ophelia would be damned proud." She grinned at Mattie and winked. "But I bet she's lookin' down from heaven right now green as hell with envy."

Mattie smiled and popped the last bite of pie into her mouth. "She taught you well, Rox, and she loved you like a daughter. She said you had a good heart."

Roxie brushed a tear from her pale cheek and smiled. "I loved the old bitch, too." She poured a splash of Tennessee whiskey into each of their cups. "Here's to Madam Ophelia, God rest her ruthless, old soul. She took no shit from any man. I hope we can do as well at this meeting of the Whiskey Row Improvement League." She lifted her cup to her lips and emptied it. "I'm goin' to bed now, Red, but I'm not lookin' forward to all those damned stairs." Mattie stood and joined her friend as they walked together out of the warm, homey kitchen.

***

Sunday morning dawned cloudy with flurries of snow dancing in the light breeze outside the Victoriana. Roxie opened her eyes to the hazy sun filtering through the colored panes of glass and sat up, keeping the warm quilt tucked up around her neck against the cold morning air.

I just can't fathom what Jim Hardy wants with us. We might be cuttin' into his business a little in the cribs, but it can't be that much and we don't sell liquor or offer gamin', so he's got no call to be after us for that. I wonder if we should ask Virgil to come along with us for protection. Surely Hardy wouldn't try anything if Virgil Earp showed up at our side.

Roxie heard her mantle clock chime ten and reluctantly pushed the quilt down to her waist and shivered. The turret room on the third floor was cold, but Roxie didn't intend to add a stove to the cramped space. Warm air moved up from the rooms down below and she and Mattie generally kept their doors open, but this morning Roxie could see her breath fog when she breathed and knew the water in her pitcher would be too cold to wash up in.

She slid into her fur-lined slippers and trudged into the privy closet to relieve herself. The little slope-ceilinged room was cold as well, and Roxie shivered as she sat on the commode chair. She stared at her reflection in the dark room and ran her fingers through her blonde waves, scratching her dry scalp with her sharp nails, tinted dark pink with henna paste.

In her room, Roxie rummaged through her wardrobe, looking for the perfect outfit to wear to the meeting with Jim Hardy and his Whiskey Row Improvement League. She tossed several onto her bed, unhappy with the lot.

Roxie finally decided on her most conservative black pinstripe suit and high-collared white silk blouse. She strolled into the warm kitchen and grinned when she saw Mattie sitting at the table dressed in her bright yellow wool.

"I look like I'm dressed for a funeral and you look like we're goin' out on a picnic," Roxie said, startling her redheaded friend as she was picking up her coffee cup.

"Do you think I should change?" Mattie asked and returned her cup to the saucer with an audible clink.

"Hell no," Roxie said as she seated herself at the round oak table and nodded to Elsie at the stove for a cup of coffee. "But I think I will. Wearin' black is probably sends the wrong message."

"I'd wear that pretty lavender suit, Miss Roxie," Elsie said as she sat the porcelain cup on the table in front of Roxie. "It brings out your eyes and the jacket rests pretty over your behind. Men like that sort of thing," the young Negro woman said with an embarrassed grin.

"She's right, Rox. You should disarm Hardy with your narrow waist and curvaceous rump."

Roxie rolled her eyes, took a sip of the hot coffee, and then stood. "Oh alright, I'll be right back." She hiked up her skirts and hurried back up the stairs to change into the lavender silk suit. She kept on the white blouse, but changed out the silver earbobs for amethyst and the jet cameo brooch for one of the dark purple stones set in gold. Roxie plucked out the jet pins from her pale, gold curls and tucked them up with plain ones. She'd wear the lavender bonnet with its purple satin ribbons and white ostrich feathers.

She stared into the oval mirror of her tall wardrobe as she pulled on a pair of white kid-skin gloves and had to agree with Elsie—the tail of this jacket *did* look nice the way it fell over the mound of her ass under the skirt and petticoat. The shade of lavender brought out the blue eyes in her pale face, as well. Roxie touched up the rouge on her lips and added a little more kohl powder to her eyelids.

Satisfied, she made her way back down the stairs and into the bright, warm kitchen. "Is this better?"

"Much," Mattie said as she sipped her coffee. "Jim Hardy's gonna be so distracted by your beauty that he's gonna forget all about whatever it was he called us down to the Palace for in the first place."

Roxie grinned and set her white fox-fur muff onto the table. "I'm bringin' this along just in the case he doesn't."

Mattie lifted her beaded bag and let it drop onto the table with a heavy metallic thunk. "Me too. I stopped by the gunsmith's the other morning and bought me one of those little Derringers you're so fond of."

"Good idea," Roxie said with a raised eyebrow, "but can you use it?"

"Cock it, point, and pull the triggers was what the gunsmith told me. I just have to be close enough and accuracy won't be much of an issue."

Roxie snorted a laugh and threw a hand to her mouth to keep from spewing coffee across the table. "That's for certain. I suppose we should take seats close up on either side of Hardy."

Mattie's face darkened. "You don't really think there's gonna be trouble, do you? Surely he wouldn't attempt violence in a public place like the Palace Hotel?"

"I don't know, Red. Hardy's an unpredictable man and I don't know what he's got on his mind with this damned meetin'. I tried to ferret out some information about this Whiskey Row Improvement League, but nobody I've talked to has ever heard of it. I went down to see Virgil, but he's never heard anything about it, either."

The clock in the parlor chimed half-past twelve. "Well," Mattie sighed and stood. "I suppose we'd better be goin. I think I'd like to walk. The cold air will do us good."

Chapter 18

November 26, 1879

They arrived in the lobby of the Palace Hotel a half an hour later with their cheeks pink from the biting cold. A man in a black waistcoat led them into the salon where several men and women sat around a long, linen-draped table. All were dressed in fashionable clothes, including the handsome dark-complected man at the head of the table, who stood as the two women entered the room.

"Good afternoon, ladies," Jim Hardy said and motioned to empty chairs on either side of his. "Won't you have seats?" He called to a waiter who stood waiting by the polished bar. "Get these ladies a hot drink Bennie. They look cold."

Roxie pulled out her chair and sat as Mattie did the same across the table. Her insides trembled and her legs felt watery, but Roxie did her best to keep her composure. "Thank you Mr. Hardy, hot coffee would be most welcome, indeed," Roxie said, turning on her honey-coated southern charm. "And what exactly can Mrs. Kirby and I do for y'all here on the Whiskey Row Improvement League?" Bennie brought them china cups and a silver pot of coffee, which he poured from, filling their cups without spilling a drop onto the white linen tablecloth.

Roxie gazed down the table, recognizing most of the other attendees. Beside her sat Thelma Joyce, a stout woman of middle age, who ran some of the cribs on Whiskey Row. Next to Mattie sat Vernon Krebb, a saloon owner on the Row and a notorious gambler. At his side sat his brother and partner, Clyde. Two other saloon owners and three prostitutes known to Roxie filled the remainder of the seats around the table. At the far end of the table sat Virgil Earp. Roxie wasn't certain if he'd been invited as a representative of Prescott's Law Commission or had simply shown up as an uninvited guest to look out for her and Mattie. For all her dislike of the Earp brothers, Roxie was glad to see his grim face and she gave him a hesitant smile.

"*You* and Mrs. Kirby," snarled Thelma, "are the whole reason for the Whiskey Row Improvement League. Your damned House is causin' us all kinds of problems."

"What kinds of problems could we possibly be causin' all y'all?" Roxie asked in her exaggerated southern drawl.

"Your high-dollar cunny," snapped one of the prostitutes dressed in a tight, red satin dress, "is cuttin' into *our* business and bringing down our profits."   ·

"And how can we possibly help you with that?" Mattie asked in exasperation as she picked up her coffee and sipped.

"You can get *out* of our business," said one of the other prostitutes who wore a faded pink dress with shabby, torn lace at the obscenely low collar. "How are we regular girls supposed to compete with you up there in that fancy place when the best we can do is the Palace here?"

Mattie smiled at the woman who looked to be younger than her by several years. "I was practicing the Trade long before you got into the business, sweetheart, and I never went complaining about any competition when it came to town. I just hitched up my skirts and got better at the business. You might try changing your nasty sheets from time to time and taking more frequent bathes with soap. Men don't like to play in other men's week-old leavings."

"Why you nasty bitch," the young woman screamed and lifted her empty glass as if to throw it at Mattie.

"She's right, Sugar," Roxie added, interrupting the girl's pitch, "We didn't hire you on at the Victoriana because when we went up to interview you in your room here it *and* you wreaked of unwashed cunny. There are whores and then there are *dirty* whores. I'm afraid you're a dirty whore, Sugar, and we don't have any of those at the Victoriana. Think on that before complanin' about why your business has dried up."

"Her business isn't the only thing that's dried up," Vernon Krebb said and the other men around the table chuckled.

Virgil cleared his throat to quiet the table. "I can understand why the whores might have a complaint with these women," he said nodding toward Mattie and Roxie, "But they don't sell spirits or have gaming tables up at their place. What bone do you fellas have to pick with them?" Virgil filled his glass with whiskey from a decanter on the table.

"We all run some girls, too," Jim Hardy said as he lit a cigar and inhaled. "And while they say they don't sell liquor, they offer it there for free and *that* definitely cuts into *our* profits." He exhaled blue smoke into the air.

"Well, there ya go, Roxie," Virgil said with an impish grin, "I guess Jim Hardy gives his blessing to you ladies *selling* spirits at the Victoriana after all."

"I never said *that*," Hardy said, glaring at the impressive muscular figure of Virgil Earp in his dark suit with his constable's badge affixed prominently to the lapel.

"Then what is it y'all want?" Roxie asked sweetly. "We specifically avoided puttin' in a saloon or gamblin' tables so as not to compete with your businesses down here on Whiskey Row, but we can't avoid at least offerin' our clients a drink if they want one." She turned to Thelma. "Tell me you don't give *your* clients a drink if they ask."

"Of course, I do," she snapped, "but that's different."

"How?" Mattie asked. "Explain to us how and we'll try to remedy it."

"I work my gals out of the Palace here or the cribs next door and I buy my liquor directly from the Hotel."

"Oh, I see," Mattie said.

"Now," Jim Hardy said, "if you ladies were prepared to pay the League here a fair percentage of your profits to offset our losses, we might be persuaded to consider this matter of your unwanted disruption of our businesses closed."

"Just how big a percentage," Roxie snapped, watching the color rise in her business partner's face.

"I don't know about you boys," Hardy said, looking down the table at the other saloon owners, "but I'd say my business is off about thirty-five percent since their brothel opened. How about you?"

"My numbers are down more than forty," snapped Thelma. "I'd need forty present on what she makes on her whores to make it right by me."

"All y'all are fucking insane," Roxie declared angrily and stood. "I'm not givin' over any of my profits just because the lot of you don't know how to deal with a little honest competition. Come on Red, we're done here."

"I couldn't agree more," Mattie said and joined her partner to walk toward the tasseled green velvet drapes that had been pulled to close the salon from the hotel's lobby.

"I wouldn't be so quick to go, ladies," Hardy said sternly, standing.

"And why would that be?" Roxie turned and asked. "Is there luncheon to go along with the demands or just some threats?"

"I don't make idle threats, woman," Hardy said in an icy tone that sent shivers down Roxie's spine.

"If you'll consider a more *reasonable* number for your extortion of our profits," Mattie said coolly, "we'll give it due consideration." She took Roxie's cold, trembling hand in hers and led her friend through the curtain and into the bustling lobby of the Palace Hotel.

"Come on, Rox, let's go into the restaurant and get something to eat. I'm starving and we can't let them think we're running away."

She tugged Roxie across the lobby and into the dining room filled with Sunday afternoon patrons dressed in their Sunday-go-to-meeting clothes. The women found seats by the window and ordered the Sunday Special of fried chicken when the waitress came by their table with glasses and a crystal pitcher of cold water.

"The bastard's gonna have us killed," Roxie said after gulping water. "But I think I'd rather be dead than pay out forty percent of our hard-earned profits to those lazy, greedy bastards. Can you believe their damned nerve?"

"I figured they might have something like that in mind," Mattie sighed, "but forty percent is a bit more than I reckoned."

"How can they possibly think we'd give up almost half our business?" Roxie motioned for the waitress and ordered a bottle of whiskey from the bar.

"It's just a starting point," Mattie said. "I'm sure they'll send around a note countering with a much lower percentage or possibly even a flat sum."

"It still galls me that we should have to pay them anything at all," Roxie snarled. "I can see havin' to pay the Law Commission in order to operate in town, but why should we have to pay the competition just because we do a better job at business than they do?"

Mattie shrugged her shoulders. "I don't know, Rox. Nobody says we *have* to pay them at all."

"Did you hear Hardy's tone? It had the cold ring of the grave to it."

The waitress brought the bottle of whiskey, but Roxie waved her away before she could pour the amber liquid into the shot glasses she'd brought along. "The son-of-a-bitch is gonna have us murdered. I just know it."

"He'll collect no profits from dead women," Mattie countered.

"Great, then we should just expect a beatin'?" Roxie filled their glasses and emptied hers in one long swallow.

Mattie furrowed her brow. "Now *that* I wouldn't put past the bastard. We should take care to not leave the house alone until this is sorted out and keep an eye on who visits. You and I shouldn't take any clients up to our rooms unless we know who they are for certain."

"That's sound advice. Do you think we should hire on some men to keep an eye out around the place?"

"Probably not a bad idea. We can ask Virgil to recommend some good men," Mattie said and Roxie saw a pensive look on her friend's face she recognized as the wheels turning in Mattie's red head. "But if we're gonna have to hire on extra men to protect us from Hardy it's gonna cost us. If the bastards don't appreciate the fact that we didn't want to horn in on their saloon business, then I suppose we ought to pay them back in kind and open up the ballroom as a full-fledge saloon and gambling hall."

"I always said you had the devious mind of a true whore, Red." Roxie gave her a sly smile and refilled her glass.

"You and my husband," Mattie sighed sadly as the waitress set plates of fried chicken, mashed potatoes with cream gravy, green beans, and biscuits onto the table in front of them.

"To hell with him, too." Roxie bit into a hot, crispy chicken leg while Mattie slathered butter onto her biscuit. "Have you heard from the son-of-a-bitch since he sold your sweet little house?"

"No, and I don't reckon I ever will. Today would have been our wedding anniversary. Three years, but he left me before we could celebrate the second."

Roxie dropped her chicken onto her plate and wiped her greasy fingers on the linen napkin. "I'm so sorry, Red, I completely forgot." She glanced absently about the dining room and then frowned. "Hell, my ninth just passed me by and I never even thought on it. It's the first time … so I guess it gets better with time."

"I suppose," Mattie sighed and scooped up mashed potatoes on her fork. "I suppose."

"So," Roxie said and poured another drink, "Where do you think we should build the bar? How many poker tables and roulette wheels? It's gonna give me some deal of pleasure to waltz from saloon to saloon on Whiskey Row poachin' dealers and their equipment away from those bastards." She gave Mattie a sly grin. "If Hardy's gonna give me a beatin', I intend to earn it." She lifted her glass in salute.

Mattie lifted hers as well. "Here, here, my friend and to hell with Jim Hardy and the Whiskey Row Improvement League."

Chapter 19

December 25, 1879

Christmas morning found the women of the Victoriana bustling around getting ready for the day's festivities. With the success of their Thanksgiving dinner, Roxie and Mattie had sent out invitations to and posted notices in most of the Prescott churches for the Christmas dinner, promising gifts from Father Christmas, as well as, the free food for all who attended.

Jessie and his father had cut a large pine that the women hung with cookies baked and decorated with colored sugar frosting by Miss Minnie, stamped tin ornaments, and strings of popped corn, which they set up in the ballroom/saloon beside the newly installed bar. The felt-topped card tables and roulette wheels had been pushed against the walls to accommodate the trestle tables and buffet counter for the dinner. As at Thanksgiving, Miss Minnie's folks had their celebration in the private dining room, which had its own festively decorated tree stacked with baskets of gifts for the women and children attending.

Roxie and Mattie had purchased a variety of small toys from Crider's, as well as oranges, rock candy, and sundry personal care items like combs, brushes, and soaps that could be stuffed into stockings and hung from the bar for the children to choose as they arrived for the dinner.

Thinking of Mr. Clayton, Mattie insisted on baskets filled with fabrics and sewing notions for the women to take home with them. It had done her heart good to see Mrs. Riley's mouth fall open as she swept the dust from her boardwalk when she and Jessie had come out of Crider's loaded down with wicker baskets, bolts of fabric in every color and weight, and boxes of toys to accompany their large order of food stuffs for the occasion. Mattie had smiled sweetly and waved as they piled the buckboard full of items that would have been purchased from Riley's had the woman not angered Mattie, destroying their business relationship.

Roxie, dressed in a bright red velvet gown looked festive beside Mattie in her green velvet.

"You look beautiful, Red. That green velvet looks divine on ya. Shall we call the girls together in the parlor?"

"Yes," Mattie said with a broad smile of anticipation. "I'll get Miss Minnie and her girls from the kitchen."

As the women of the Victoriana sat before the blazing fire in the parlor's fireplace, Mattie passed around the brightly wrapped packages she'd worked on the night before. Some of the girls had packages to exchange and most had small items for Mattie, Roxie, and Miss Minnie as well.

With all the packages distributed, Mattie took a seat in one of the wingback chairs and began to open the ones for her. This signaled the others and the ripping of paper and giggles filled the parlor.

"Oh, Miss Mattie," Minnie said as she held up the silver-framed hand mirror in one wrinkled, brown hand and one of the little scent bottles in the other. "This here is way too much for an old woman like me."

"Not at all," Mattie sighed. "You deserve so very much more."

"We thank you with all our hearts," gushed Minnie as her daughter and granddaughter held up identical silver pieces. "It's all so very lovely."

"They'll look nice in all our rooms," Roxie said as she sat fondling the stiff boar's bristles of her own brush. "What do you think of yours, Red?"

Mattie sat with a wicker basket upon her knees with hinged lids to keep in the contents. She opened it and smiled. Inside were new fabric sheers, pins, needles, and a variety of colorful spools of sewing thread.

"I love it. Now I can get started on those new frillies I've been thinkin' on," she said with a giggle.

Moira stood and carried a package to set at Mattie's feet. "Open dis one next, Miss Mattie. 'Tis from de lot of us," she said and motioned to the other women.

Mattie pulled the green satin ribbon to release the paper and her eyes went wide. Her hands brushed over a folded piece of white cotton fabric embroidered with white silk thread in the shape of vines and flowers. A pile of broad white crocheted silk lace and narrow white satin ribbon lie piled atop the fabric.

"This is beautiful fabric," Mattie said, batting back tears.

"It'll make some beautiful frillies," Martha offered with a broad grin.

"There's enough fabric here to make a complete set with a camisole, bloomers, and a petticoat with lots of lace," Mattie gasped.

"And we'll be expecting you to model them for us when you're finished with them," Roxie said with a bright smile.

Roxie's package from the girls contained a set of frillies from the same fabric already made by Mrs. Clayton and her sewing machine. Roxie's white fabric was decorated with blue silk embroidery and blue ribbons accented the white lace.

"These are beautiful," Roxie said, holding up the pair of bloomers with their thick rows of bright white lace at the cuffs. "Thank you all ever so much."

The house smelled of Christmas. Pine boughs decorated with peppermint canes and cinnamon cookies hung from the banisters. Turkeys and hams roasted in the kitchen and the aroma of spicy sweet potato pies filled the air. The big trees in the dining rooms were heaped high with gifts for the attendees.

By two in the afternoon bellies had been filled and the orchestra had switched from mellow carols to livelier dance tunes and waltzes. Tables had been cleared from the dance floor to be replaced by laughing couples twirling in one another's arms. Children sat upon the floor playing with things from their stockings. Boys raced their carved wooden horses and girls compared and traded the clothes on their rag dolls.

Mattie and Roxie sat in the parlor as Mrs. Pearce, the minister's wife came in, staring around the room. She had a younger woman with her, holding a small child by the hand.

"Where is your outhouse?" Mrs. Pearce asked.

"We have a privy closet just there," Mattie said and pointed to a door beneath the wide stairs.

Mrs. Pearce pushed the young woman toward the door just as a Negro woman with a child of about the same age came walking out to return to the dining room where lively fiddle and banjo music could be heard.

"You have Negroes here?" Mrs. Pearce gasped. "And you're allowing them to use the same facilities as the whites?"

"You're more than welcome to use the outhouse by the stables in the cold if you'd prefer," Roxie said, pointing toward the back of the house.

"I should have expected nothing better from the likes of you in this low place of Satan, but I'd have thought a Southern woman like yourself would have better sense about mixing the races," Mrs. Pearce snarled and nudged the woman with the little boy toward the kitchen and the back door.

The younger woman turned her head and mouthed, "I'm sorry."

"I suppose Minnie was right," Roxie said sadly.

"It's sad to say," Mattie agreed. "But I think everything else is going just beautifully."

Roxie poured two glasses of whiskey and handed one to Mattie. "I think so, too. The children are certainly enjoying themselves." High pitched laughter floated down from the ballroom.

"Don't get your dander up about the preacher's wife, Rox. There has to be one in every crowd," Mattie said and sipped her whiskey. "But I bet the bitch will be back next time for the free food."

"I've no doubt of that," Roxie agreed.

A few hours later people began to filter out of the house. Mattie tapped Roxie's shoulder as the Reverend and Mrs. Pearce were leaving. They both carried two gift baskets of fabric, each piled to the handles with stockings of children's gifts, though they only had the one child, who carried two of his own.

"Maybe they're takin' them for families from the church that couldn't come," Mattie said.

"Yah," Roxie huffed and rolled her eyes incredulously, "and I'm the Virgin Mother."

"I'll give them the benefit of the doubt," Mattie said softly and shrugged her shoulders.

"You're a better woman than me, Red."

The young woman who'd been with Mrs. Pearce came into the parlor and offered her hand to Mattie and Roxie in turn.

"Thank you for this party," she said. "My name is Lydia Ryan and if it weren't for you, me and my boy wouldn't have had a Christmas to speak of this year." The little boy carried a stocking clutched close to his frail body and had a carved wooden horse in his other hand as he leaned close into his mother's skirt. "And I want to apologize for the Reverend's wife's rudeness earlier. She's a bit high-strung."

"Are you staying with the Pearces?" Mattie asked.

Her question was answered when Mrs. Pearce stuck her head into the door. "Come Lydia we're ready to go. We need to get home so you can get the food put away before bed."

Mattie glanced down into Lydia's basket and saw two pies covered with linen napkins piled atop the folded fabric and sewing notions.

"Yes, ma'am," Lydia called back.

"Unless, of course, you're applying for a job," the preacher's wife snapped before popping back out the door.

"I'm coming," Lydia called and then turned back to Mattie and Roxie. "I'm sorry. My husband died of the cholera last summer and the Pearces took us in."

"Momma's a maid now," the little boy offered.

"Maid, cook, laundress, and stable hand," Lydia sighed and began walking toward the door.

"If we invite the Reverend Pearce's church back," Roxie whispered to Mattie, "make certain we assign a girl to watch them so they don't leave with anything more than anyone else."

"If she had two pies in her basket," Mattie said aghast, "how much more do you think they walked out with?"

"Enough to feed the Reverend and his wife for the next week, I'm certain," Roxie said, shaking her blonde head.

"Not to mention our linens and dishes."

"I'll have Minnie make a count tomorrow," Roxie said sadly. "Do you think other people did the same?"

Mattie shrugged her shoulders. "I hate to think so, but if church folks would steal, then I wouldn't put it past others."

"Especially if they saw the good church folks doin' the stealin'."

"Come on, Rox," Mattie said and put an arm around her friend's slender, velvet-clad waist, "let's go see if Mrs. Pearce left us any pie."

Chapter 20

January 12, 1880

Roxie sat in the dining room of the Palace Hotel enjoying a late lunch when someone tapped her on the shoulder. She looked up to see a stylishly dressed Alan Ramsay standing beside her table.

"Hello, Mr. Ramsay," she said. "How very nice to see you again."

"May I be so bold as to ask to join you, Miss Roxie?"

Roxie glanced around the busy dining room. Several sets of eyes watched them and Roxie motioned toward the empty chair across from her. "Please," she said sweetly."

Ramsay adjusted his black silk trousers and sat. "Why are you dining alone?" He asked as he sat.

Roxie smiled and let her eyes dart around the room. "I'm a whore, Mr. Ramsay. I'm not considered fit company for Sunday dinner."

"Nonsense," he said. "You're a beautiful woman. You shouldn't be sitting here eating alone."

Roxie felt her cheeks begin to burn. She smiled at the handsome man and suddenly considered him in a new light. "Why, thank you, sir. That's ever so kind of you to say."

A young waitress came rushing to the table. She carried a crystal glass filled with water and set it before Alan Ramsay. "What can I get for you Mr. Ramsay, sir?" Roxie watched the waitress glance down at her and then around the crowded dining room. "Can I find you a more … a more suitable table, sir?" The young woman stumbled over her words as she nervously avoided Roxie.

Ramsay glared up at the jittery waitress. "I wouldn't be sitting here if I didn't want to be," he snapped and smiled at Roxie. "I'm sitting with the most beautiful woman in Prescott. Why would I want another table?"

"Yes, sir, of course sir," she mumbled. "What can I get for you today?"

"I'll have my usual," he said curtly, "and a whiskey from the saloon." He glanced at Roxie's half-empty glass. "Bring the lady another of whatever she's drinking as well."

"Yes sir," she said and scurried away.

"You're a regular here, I gather," Roxie said and picked up her glass.

"It's the only place in town where I can get a decent meal *and* a whiskey," he said with a broad smile. "How are things at your house? I heard you put on quite the do for Christmas."

"You heard about that?" Roxie said in surprise.

Ramsay raised a thick black eyebrow. "I hear about most everything that goes on in Prescott." His face darkened and he asked, "How are things going with you and the Whiskey Row Improvement League?"

"You know about that too?" Roxie gasped.

"James Hardy and I are … acquainted." Ramsay picked up the crystal glass and sipped. "Are you expecting trouble from him?"

"I certainly hope not," Roxie sighed.

The frowning waitress returned with their whiskeys. "Mr. Ramsay, sir," she said as she set the shot glasses on the table, "there's a gentleman in the saloon who'd like you to join him there."

Alan Ramsay glowered up at her. "Tell whoever it is that I'm having my dinner and enjoying the company of a lovely lady. He can wait or he can come in and speak to here."

She bobbed her head. "Yes, sir, I'll tell him."

Ramsay shook his head and picked up his whiskey. "I'll always choose the company of a beautiful woman over that of some fool in the saloon."

Roxie lifted her glass. "Why thank you, sir. That's ever so kind of you to say."

"I've been thinking about you since ..." He hesitated and Roxie saw color flood his cheeks. "Well since our last encounter." He gulped some water. "You've been on my mind a good bit and ..."

"I thought you'd at least have the courtesy to join me for a drink, Ramsay," someone growled and Roxie looked away from Ramsay to see James Hardy standing beside their table. He glared down at Roxie. "I certainly thought you had more respect than to snub me for the company of a thieving whore."

Roxie heard snickering from around the dining room and didn't look up. The addition of a gaming hall and saloon in the ballroom of The Victoriana had probably cut into Hardy's profits down here on Whiskey Row and she grinned. Business had been good in their new addition.

"There's no need to be rude, Jim," Ramsay said in a calm voice. "I told the girl to tell you I was having my dinner and I'd be more than happy join you for a drink later."

"Don't bother," Hardy sneered, "if you prefer the company of this dirty slut to mine." He turned and stormed out of the dining room with all the eyes of the assembled patrons following his stout frame.

"Young woman," Roxie heard the high nasal voice of a female ask, "Why do you tolerate such filth in your dining room?" Roxie looked up to see Mrs. Pearce and her severely dressed husband, the Reverend Pearce, sitting at a nearby table. "We're good Christian folk just come from services and we shouldn't have to share a room with such godless trash as *her*," Mrs. Pearce sneered and glared across the room at Roxie.

Roxie's felt her cheeks burning and she dropped her hands to the tabletop and started to rise, but Ramsay snatched up her hand from across the table. She glanced up at him and smiled, her anger abating with his warm touch.

"Just ignore the old shrew," Ramsay said softly as he squeezed her trembling hand. "She's just jealous of such a beautiful woman."

The Reverend and Mrs. Pearce scooted back their chairs noisily and stood. Roxie saw the empty plates on their table and a mischievous grin spread across her pale face.

"Sugar," Roxie called to the dumbfounded waitress in a loud, but sweet southern drawl, "you'd best check that one's bag." Roxie pointed to Mrs. Pearce. "She's quite fond of carryin' home other folk's tableware."

Mrs. Pearce gaped at Roxie. "Why, I never ..." she gasped, took her husband's elbow, and stormed out of the dining room followed by tittering laughter.

"You're an amazing woman," Ramsay said with a broad smile as he tightened the grip on Roxie's hand. "I don't think I've ever known a woman quite like you."

Roxie blushed. "Why thank you, sir," she said and batted her big blue eyes.

"I'd be honored if you'd call me Alan," he said as their waitress brought plates of pan-fried steak and mashed potatoes covered in cream gravy to set in front of them.

Roxie's cheeks continued to burn. She hadn't felt this caddywampus in a long time. Her heart fluttered in her chest as she stared at the handsome man across the table from her.

He's a client, Roxanna. Stop actin' like one of those ridiculous school girls in your silly dime-novels.

"As I was saying before Jim interrupted me, I've been thinking about you ever since ..." He hesitated and Roxie watched as color flooded his cheeks again. "Well since I saw you last." His eyes darted nervously around the room. "I've been meaning to visit again, but without ... uh ... without Dewey." He emptied his whiskey glass.

"It would be my pleasure to see you again, Alan," Roxie said as she cut her steak. "I'm available after five any day."

He's just a damned client. She popped the bite of steak into her mouth and chewed. *Just a damned client.*

"I thought to ask you to dinner," he said, hesitantly. "I didn't know if you'd be willing to see me socially." He raised an eyebrow. "Do you do that?" He queried. "Do you see men socially or only for business?"

Roxie swept a hand over the table. "I'm seein' y'all now. This is social and not business, isn't it?" The words flew from her lips sharper than she'd intended. "I'm sorry, Alan. I didn't mean to be curt. It's been a nerve-wrackin' afternoon."

"Jim ... or that sour old bitch?" He asked with a grin.

"Both, I guess," Roxie sighed and sipped her whiskey.

"Are you worried about Jim and his bunch of cronies?"

Roxie took a deep breath. "Truthfully, I suppose I am. He scares me some."

"Jim Hardy scares everybody some," Ramsay said with a grin, "It's how he's wrangled his position here on Whiskey Row. He's a bully and a blowhard." Ramsay took a bite of his steak. "I don't think he'll do you any harm … not if you pay him what he wants, anyway."

"Well," Roxie growled, "we're surely not gonna give the son-of-a-bitch forty percent of our profits." She forked up some potatoes and put them into her mouth.

"He wants forty percent?" Ramsay said, wide-eyed. "Are you serious?"

"He'll probably want more now that we've added the gamblin' hall and saloon upstairs," she said with a broad grin. "We didn't open with one, but when he and his Whiskey Row Improvement League called us down here and made their ridiculous demands," she said and shrugged her shoulders, "me and Red said, what the hell, and added one."

"How's it going for you?" He asked and bit into a buttered biscuit.

Roxie hesitated and then grinned. "Hardy and Krebb can't be very happy. The booze and our cut of the tables are bringin' in as much as the girls," she said and sipped her whiskey, "and the girls are bringin' in more than before we opened it."

"Sounds to me like Hardy and his Whiskey Row Improvement League shot themselves in the foot."

"I think you might be right." Roxie looked up to see Virgil Earp and his wife standing by the table.

Allie Earp stood nervously at her husband's side dressed in a heavy polonaise against the winter cold. Her golden-brown hair looked almost the same shade as the fur at her collar and cuffs. She smiled down at Roxie and gave her a thin, nervous smile. "I hear business is good, Rox. I'm happy for you."

Roxie stared up at the pretty woman in surprise. "Thank you, Allie. I appreciate it and I'll pass your thoughts along to Mattie."

"How's she doing?" Allie asked sincerely. "I haven't seen her in a while. I know Doc Robinson misses her help something fierce."

"She misses helpin' him out," Roxie replied, "but business is good and we need her at The Victoriana."

Allie Earp bent and spoke softly to Roxie. "I've been dying to see the place. We wanted to come up for one of your parties, but ..." Roxie saw the woman's big brown eyes lift to nervously scan the busy dining room.

"I understand," Roxie sighed and took Allie's gloved hand. "Why don't you pay a call early in the day for coffee some time. I know Red would be proud to see you and we'll give you the grand tour."

"Is Miss Minnie still cooking for you?" Allie asked. "She was the only reason I ate in that horrid man's café and I haven't been back since you stole her away from him."

"Isn't she just a gem?" Roxie said with a smile. "She, her daughter, and her granddaughter work for us. We're very lucky to have them."

"Come on woman," Virgil said and tugged at his wife. "I'm starvin'."

Alan Ramsay touched the sleeve of Virgil's brown wool jacket to stop him before he could walk away. "Have you heard Krebb or Hardy make any overt threats against the women at The Victoriana, Virgil?"

Virgil's dark eyes darted to Roxie. "You and Mattie should take care, Roxie," he warned. "Did you hire any of those fellas I recommended to you?"

"Parker Hudson and Carson McKenna," she said.

"They're both good fellas," Virgil said with a nod. "Keep a close eye on her, Alan," he said, looking back to Ramsay, "I don't trust Hardy and that cow Thelma is almost as bad. I wouldn't put it past her to take a shot at Roxie or Mattie if she had the chance. Krebb is trying to use the law to get the place shut down, but Hardy is more of a brute force kinda fella." He looked back to Roxie with concern etched on his dark face. "You and Mattie watch yourselves."

"Thank you, Virgil, we will," Roxie said as the couple walked to an empty table.

Ramsay reached across the table and took Roxie's hand. "I'd be proud to escort you home, Roxie."

Roxie stared at the items on a tray their waitress carried to another table. "Maybe after a piece of that pie and some coffee," she said and smiled at the handsome man sitting across from her. "I'd be happy for your company on the walk back home … Alan."

Chapter 21

March 3, 1880

Mattie sat with Roxie and Allie Earp in the parlor of the Victoriana sipping coffee when Moira came rushing in, her cheeks red from the cold and exertion. She sat panting and hugging her shawl around her tightly.

"Whatever is it, Moira?" Roxie asked as she poured a cup of hot coffee to press into the girl's cold, trembling hand. "You look like you've seen a ghost."

Moira jerked her reed head up to stare at Roxie. "I think I did," she muttered, almost to herself.

"What?" Mattie asked with her eyes flitting to Roxie's. "What is it that has you in such a panic, Moira?"

Allie Earp sat quietly, sipping her coffee as Roxie and Mattie attended to their young employee.

"It was Pete," Moira finally blurted. "I was walking downtown and saw him comin' out of The Peacock just as bold as ya please." She gulped some hot coffee before continuing. "He walks with a limp now and his face sags a bit on the left," she said and lifted as hand to her left cheek that had gone pale, "but I swear to the good lord it was him."

"I thought that son-of-a-bitch was down in the Territorial prison in Yuma," Roxie said to Mattie.

"So did I," Mattie replied and set her cup of coffee on the side table. They only gave him a six-month sentence. I suppose it's been all of that."

"If he's enfeebled," Allie offered, "perhaps they gave him an early release." She refilled her delicate china cup from the pot. "Virgil is always saying the Territory is short of funds," she shrugged her shoulders imperceptively. "Perhaps they simply couldn't afford his care and turned him out."

"I suppose that makes sense," Mattie said and refilled her cup as well. "Did he see you, Moira?"

"Oh, no, ma'am," Moira gasped and shook her head. "I stopped dead in me … eh … my tracks and waited for him to go on his way and he didn't see me."

Mattie smiled at the girl's quick correction of her grammar. She and Roxie had been pressing Moira to lose her Irish accent as much as possible and the girl had been doing an admirable job. A few men enjoyed hearing the accent of the Old Country, but Roxie ranted about not wanting her girls to be thought of as low-rent Irish cunnies. There was plenty of that in the cribs down on Whisky Row. The Victoriana had higher standards.

"It's no matter," Mattie said with a confidant smile. "He probably wouldn't have recognized you anyway. You're a healthy, beautiful, young woman now and not that dirty, skinny waif we found on the side of the road."

Mattie watched Moira run her hands over the bright blue wool skirt and smile. "Yes, ma'am. I've come a long way since then."

Roxie stood and took Moira by the hand. "Let's go upstairs and pick out something pretty for you to wear tonight." She turned to Allie and smiled warmly. "Thanks for stoppin' by, Allie. It was ever so nice to see ya again."

Allie stood as well. "I suppose I should be going, as well," she said and slipped into her fur-trimmed coat. "Thank you, Mattie for showing me the place. It's everything I expected it to be." Allie gave her an impish grin and added, "Bessie will be absolutely green with envy. I can't wait to tell her every little detail."

"You're an evil woman, Allie Earp," Mattie said and returned the grin. "You should bring her by the next time she's in town."

Allie rolled her big brown eyes and gave Mattie a hug. "Only if I can bring along a photographer to catch the look on her face."

Mattie returned her hug and showed Allie to the door. "Would you mind asking Virgil to check into that early release? The bastard doesn't scare me any, but Moira's frightened of him and I don't think much of the fact that he was coming out of James Hardy's place when she saw him." Mattie stood on the porch enjoying the early March sunshine. "We just don't need that kind of trouble."

"Don't fret on it, Mattie," Allie said and patted Mattie's hand before walking down the wide stairs toward the drive and her waiting buggy. "I'll ask Virgil to look into it." She waved to Mattie and strolled to her buggy, climbed in, and urged to horse off down the street.

Mattie stood enjoying the sunshine for a few more minutes before returning to the parlor where Minnie stood collecting the coffee service.

"Was you all finished with this, Miss Mattie or did you want some more?"

"I'm fine, Minnie, thank you." Mattie looked around. "Why are you collecting the dirty dishes, Minnie? Where's your daughter?" She rushed over to take the china-laden tray from the elderly woman. "You're our cook," Mattie chided, "not our maid."

"I sent the girls to Crider's for the grocery order," Minnie explained. "I'm not so old I can't carry a tray of dirty saucers to the kitchen," she grumbled under her breath.

Mattie deposited the tray on the kitchen table and turned to a frowning Miss Minnie. "I know that, Miss Minnie, I just don't want you to take on more than necessary." Mattie put her arm around the Negro cook's shoulders and pulled her close. "You do more than your share out here in the kitchen."

"Oh, Miss Mattie," the old woman said and shrugged Mattie's arm away to pick up the tray and carry it to the sink. "You pay me good and put a nice roof over my head. Me and my girls appreciate all you and Miss Roxie do for us."

"Nonsense," Mattie said as the knocker on the big oak door sounded. "I'll get it," she called and turned to walk back toward the entryway.

Mattie opened the door to find Mr. Grady standing on the porch in his blue cap and suit. "I have a telegram for you Mrs. Kirby unless there's a harlot residing here by the name of Mattie Wallace and she's not you," he said snidely as his eyes stared past her to get a look inside the elegant brothel.

Mattie snatched the envelope from his hand when he offered it. "Thank you, Mr. Grady. I'm sure it's for me," she said curtly before slamming the door in his expectant face without offering a tip.

"Who was that?" Roxie asked as she came down the stairs.

"Just that ass Grady," Mattie huffed and lifted the envelope for Roxie to see as she carried it back into the parlor. "Mattie Wallace got a telegram."

"You haven't been Mattie Wallace in several years," Roxie said as she followed her friend. "Who do you think it's from?"

Mattie took a seat in one of the wingback chairs in front of the fireplace. "Well, let's have a look," she said and ripped open the envelope. She scanned it quickly and then read it out loud to Roxie.

3, March 1880

Office of Harold Shanks, Attorney, Phoenix

Miss Wallace,

I have been hired as a representative of the estate of the late James Devaroe of St. Louis, Missouri. As such, I will be arriving in Prescott within the week to make a presentation to you of the items bequeathed to you in his will.

Until then, my condolences at your loss.

Harold Shanks

"James is dead?" Roxie said and dropped into the other chair. "I wonder what happened."

"I wonder how he knew I was in Arizona," Mattie said and folded the hand-written message to set on the table between their chairs.

"Well," Roxie said and cleared her throat nervously. "I may have let him know about that."

"You?" Mattie said gaping, wide-eyed at her little friend. "You never mentioned being in touch with James Devaroe."

"I had a letter from him not long after Ophelia's death," Roxie admitted as she stood and walked to pour a glass of Tennessee Whisky from a crystal decanter on a shelf by the fireplace. "He was her silent business partner at The Palace, you know. She'd left me a few dollars in her will and he mailed me the funds." She handed Mattie a glass and then took a long swallow of hers. "We exchanged letters for a while and I told him you'd gotten married and moved here to Prescott." She shrugged her petite shoulders. "Maybe I never told him your married name or he just forgot it. When we opened the Victoriana, I wrote and let him know we were doing it together. I guess that's how his lawyers knew where to find you." She took another long swallow. "James was only five years older than me," Roxie sighed. "I wonder what happened. Forty is too damned young to just fall over dead."

"He lived hard, Rox," Mattie said, noting the stress the news of Devaroe's death was causing her friend. "Maybe it was an accident on one of his boats. You know he wasn't the sort to just sit back and let others do the heavy lifting. How many times did we see him up on deck with the crew moving freight around or going down to the engine room to help work on a boiler?"

"You're probably right," Roxie sighed. "And he played cards with a pretty rough group. He may have gotten himself shot across the poker table."

"Or stabbed by a woman," Mattie added, remembering her rough night with him at Madam Ophelia's Palace all those years ago. "I'm sure he deserved whatever he got, in any case."

Roxie raised her glass with the shadow of a smile on her pretty face. "I'm sure he did," she said. "I guess we'll just have to wait until that Phoenix lawyer shows up to find out what it was."

***

Two days after the arrival of the telegram from Harrold Shanks, the man himself knocked on the door of the Victoriana in a brown tweed jacket and wool trousers. A bowler hat set cocked atop his balding head and gold-rimmed spectacles rested on the bridge of his squat nose.

Jessie answered the door and showed him into the parlor where Mattie and Roxie sat with the women of the Victoriana discussing items in a recent copy of The San Francisco Chronicle. The man's mouth fell open as he gazed about the room at the women sitting in their frillies and dressing gowns.

"Pardon me … ladies," he said stumbling over his words nervously, "I'm here … eh … to speak with a Miss Mattie Wallace." His eyes scanned the tittering group of women. "Is she amongst you?"

Mattie grinned as the man tried to shift his weight to hide the bulge that had grown in the front of his trousers. She stood and her dressing gown fell open to reveal her corset and bloomers. "It's Mattie Kirby now," she said and stepped forward with her hand extended.

Harold Shanks took her hand and tried; without success, to avoid staring at Mattie's ample cleavage over the top of her white corset. "I sent you a wire on the third," he said, red-faced.

"I received it," she said and gathered her dressing gown up and pulled the tie tight at the waist. "Let's go into the kitchen to talk. Will you join us Roxie?"

"Wouldn't miss it for the world," Roxie said and followed them into the kitchen where Minnie and her girls were busy cleaning up from breakfast.

"Minnie would you pour Mr. Shanks a cup of coffee? Mr. Shanks can we offer you something to eat? Miss Minnie makes the best fruit tarts you'd ever want to put in your mouth."

"I could certainly do with a tart," he said and his face reddened even deeper as he realized the pun.

"We have tarts in abundance in this house, sir," Minnie said with a wink at Mattie as she set a glass plate of fruit-filled pastries on the table along with a fresh pot of coffee.

Harold shanks set his hat upon the table and picked up his coffee. "As I noted in my telegram, Miss … eh … Mrs."

"Kirby," Mattie said.

"Yes," Shanks stammered, "Mrs. Kirby. I'm here representing the estate of the late James Eduard Devaroe of St. Louis."

"What happened to him?" Roxie blurted as she splashed some Tennessee whisky into her coffee cup from her silver flask. "Do you know?"

"Just a moment," the lawyer said and opened his brown leather valise. He rustled through the contents and brought out a bundle of papers. He sorted through those and pulled out a large envelope. From that he withdrew a folded newspaper clipping. "I took the liberty of bringing this along. His attorney in New Orleans sent it to me." He handed Roxie the article. "Your friend was murdered by pirates in the south seas," he said.

"I'll be damned," Roxie gasped as she stared at the clipping. "James Devaroe was killed by fucking pirates?"

"Yes, ma'am," Shanks said and cleared his throat. "It seems Mr. Devaroe had expanded his shipping concerns into Asia and was transporting Celestials from China to San Francisco when his ship was commandeered and he was killed."

"Well, I'll be damned," Roxie said again and added more whisky to her cup. She offered some to Shanks who nudged his cup toward her thankfully.

"What else do you have for me?" Mattie asked and took a sip of her coffee.

"Oh, yes," Shanks said and rustled through the papers some more. "Here you go," he said and handed Mattie a sealed envelope. Mattie Wallace was written in a flowery script.

Mattie opened the envelope and pulled out a folded sheet of heavy paper. The same flowing script covered the page.

10, July, 1879

Little Whore,

Mattie read and frowned. It was what he'd called her on that night he'd paid for her company at Madam Ophelia's. He'd brutalized her that night and Mattie had hated him for years afterward.

But I understand from Roxanna that you are no longer just a little whore, but a Madam in a luxurious brothel. I commend you on your determination. I had hoped that my ill treatment would have dissuaded you from that path, but I see it did not.

Roxanna also told me of your marriage, as well as the birth and subsequent loss of both your husband and child. Having suffered the loss of my sweet wife, Olivia, I mourn with you. My children, however, survive and live on their grandparents' sugar plantation in Louisiana. You will perhaps recall my friend Armand Thibodeaux. I married his very lovely daughter and we had twins; a boy and a girl.

No matter how luxurious, I know the life of a whore is bound to be a short one. With that thought in mind and at the urging of my sweet Olivia to make amends with you for my ill treatment, I have decided to leave you my house on Tucker Street in St. Louis for your retirement. My children do not want it. Winters in St. Louis do not agree with them overmuch.

Perhaps you will want to remain in Arizona. If such is the case, you can sell the Tucker Street house. It is in a desirable neighborhood and should bring a good price. I'm certain the attorney handling my estate would be happy to assist you with the sale if you should so desire.

If the simple news of my demise does not bring you joy, then I hope my small gift will. I wish you well Little Whore and hope you can find a small place in your heart to forgive my ill treatment of you all those years ago. I am truly sorry.

James Eduard Devaroe, Sr.

A tear slipped from Mattie's eye and she wiped it away as she handed Roxie the letter.

Chapter 22

May 11, 1880

"Damnit," Roxie cursed as she snagged her finger on another thorn. She wanted roses for the mantle in the parlor and the red ones were finally blooming. She'd already cut eight nice stems, but had just as many scratches from the devilishly sharp thorns.

Red's right, I should stop bein' a tight-wad and hire a gardener for this sort of thing.

"Those are pretty, Roxie," Mattie said from the porch. "Alan's gonna love them."

"I'm cuttin' them for the mantle in the parlor, not my room."

"Uh huh," Mattie said with an impish grin. "And I suppose that special steak supper you ordered from Miss Minnie is just for me and you?"

"Oh, hush," Roxie scolded. "A girl's gotta eat." She clipped one more rose, added it to her bundle and held them out in front of her to admire. "They are especially pretty this year, don't ya think?" She brought them up under her nose and inhaled. "Smell especially sweet too."

"It's half past three," Mattie chided, if you don't get in here and take your bath your hair won't be dry before Alan gets here."

"Oh my word, Roxie gasped, "Is it that late already?" She handed the bundle of fragrant flowers up to Mattie. "Will you put these in water for me?" Roxie tugged off her straw sun bonnet and rushed up the stairs. "Keep one out for our supper tray, though," she said before she disappeared through the front door and into the Victoriana.

Alan Ramsay had become a regular visitor to the Victoriana and Roxie's bed since their lunch together at the Palace. He'd taken her to visit his new house being built to the southwest of Prescott and she and Mattie had put him in touch with some of their suppliers and finish carpenters for his project. As much as it galled both Mattie and Roxie to refer him to any of the Meyers' relatives, they had to admit her brother was one of the best in the area.

Virgil Earp still held an interest in the local sawmill and Roxie talked Alan into purchasing the remainder of his finish lumber from there. Virgil had checked into the circumstances of Pete's early release from the prison in Yuma and Allie had been correct. His ongoing medical issues from the cracked skull he received from Minnie had prompted prison officials to grant him an early release on medical grounds, though only a few weeks early.

Bessie and James Earp had yet to visit Prescott again, so Allie was not able to show off the Victoriana to her and point out how much more beautiful it was than Bessie's tawdry house in Dodge City had been. Roxie and Mattie heard scraps of news about the Earps and their exploits down in Tombstone from customers, Alan, and Virgil. Morgan and Wyatt seemed to be in a running dispute with some ranchers and supposed cattle thieves by the name of Clanton. Virgil hoped it wouldn't blow up in their faces, but knowing both their tempers and stubborn streaks, Roxie didn't hold out much hope of a good ending. Wyatt finally got tired of the laudanum-addicted Mattie Blaylock and set her aside for some actress he met in one of the dancehalls.

That piece of news came by way of the whore's news network. Working women traveled and their news about other whores and their clients traveled with them. Women travel north in the summers to work in Prescott and Flagstaff. They traveled back south in the winter.

Katie wrote occasionally, but her letters were generally incoherent and smelled of cheap whisky. Doc had opened a dentistry practice in Tombstone, but spent more time at the card tables or working as a deputy for the Earps that it had floundered very soon after opening. Katie's letters were generally filled with cursing Doc and his gambling, Doc and his whoring, Doc and his drinking; and Doc and the Earps. She talked about leaving Tombstone to work in Bisbee, or Globe, or Tucson. She even talked about coming back to Prescott, but Roxie honestly couldn't fathom that ever happening. Katie was glued to the consumptive dentist and Roxie didn't think they'd ever part until his lungs finally failed him.

Maybe when Doc is gone, I'll invite her here to stay with Mattie and me at the Victoriana. Prescott might be a good place for her to retire to.

Roxie washed her hair, toweled it good, and left it down to dry. Alan liked it down better than pinned up, anyhow. She dressed in her blue eyelet frillies and her blue dressing gown. It was very casual, but she knew Alan would want her out of them and on her knees in front of the mirror soon after their supper. He was a man of simple tastes, but predictable. She ran her silver comb through her damp curls one last time before heading downstairs to check with Miss Minnie about their supper. Alan would be arriving around five as the Victoriana opened for the evening.

She walked through the gambling hall where Minnie's granddaughter was busy filling trays with food customers could eat with their fingers like slices of ham or beef and cheese between slices of fresh bread, pork ribs in a sweet glaze, chunks of fruit, and of course Miss Minnie's wonderful bite-size sweet treats. Both Roxie and Mattie were of the opinion more men in Prescott visited the Victoriana for Miss Minnie's cooking than either the gambling or the girls.

Most of the tables stood empty. The dealers didn't show up with their cards until after five when the house officially opened for business, but a couple were open for early business, as were a couple of girls. The girls rotated the early shift and it had quickly become popular.

One man stood at the bar and when he caught sight of Roxie in the big mirror behind the bar he pushed away and rushed toward her. "Hey there, gorgeous," he said and grabbed Roxie by her arm and pulled her into a seat at an empty table. He yanked her dressing gown open and leered at her milky-white bosoms mounded above her corset.

"Good afternoon, Mr. Dewey," Roxie said politely. "You're in early today."

He ran a rough finger over the lacy top edge of her corset, just brushing her skin. "You dress up just for me?" He asked and licked his full lips. "Why don't you and me go up to that room of yours and you can give me a little of what Al got the last time." He dropped his beefy hand to between her legs and began exploring her bloomers for access. "Ah, there it is," he sighed when he found the opening between her legs and worked his hand inside her bloomers.

"I actually have a previous appointment for this evening, Mr. Dewey," Roxie said, but relaxed her legs to allow him access to her cunny. She didn't want the man to rip her bloomers. "I'm sure one of the other girls would be more than happy to accommodate you. Joanna perhaps?"

Roxie felt a finger shove into her cunny and begin to rotate. "I don't want Joanna's used up ass," he sneered. "Al went on for weeks about your tight little asshole and I want that." With his free hand he dug into his pocket and slapped a gold piece onto the green felt tabletop. "There's your twenty," he said with breath that smelled of stale beer. He repositioned his hand and found her anus. "I want my cock sliding in and out of that," he slurred as he jammed his finger into Roxie.

Roxie flinched and tried to stand. "I'm sorry, Mr. Dewey, but I'm not takin' clients tonight."

Dewey's face changed from one of joviality to something much darker. He gripped her harder between the legs and forced his thumb into her cunny and another finger into her ass. "Hardy's right," he growled, "You're just another lyin', thievin' whore." He gripped her hard and Roxie felt his thumb nail dig into the soft tissue of her tender cunny.

"Please, Mr. Dewey," Roxie gasped, "you're hurting me."

Dewey reached up, wrapped a hand around one of her bosoms, and began to squeeze hard. "Bitch," he growled, "you don't know what hurt is yet. When Jim Hardy and his boys are done with ya not even a mange-ridden dog or injun will want to fuck ya."

"John, would you be so kind as to take your hands off my lady?" Roxie jerked her head up to see Alan Ramsay standing beside them and staring at Dewey's hand between her legs.

Dewey released her breast. "Your what?" He asked incredulously with wide eyes. "Don't tell me this little bitch has you caught in the honey-trap between her legs, Alan." He glared at Roxie and dug his thumb nail in a little deeper. "Makes no never mind really. Hardy and his boys have plans for her, the redheaded cunny, and this place." He pulled his hand from between Roxie's legs, waved it over his head to indicate The Victoriana, and stood. "I'd steer clear of 'em all Alan. It ain't gonna be good for anybody's health to be around 'em." He put his finger under his nose, inhaled deeply, and smiled before storming away.

"Are you alright?" Alan asked as he took a seat beside Roxie.

"What do you think he meant about Hardy and his *boys*?" Roxie asked as she stared around the empty gambling hall. "Where is everybody? This place is usually crowded by now." She moved her eyes from one gaming table to another and stood. "None of my dealers are here either." She took Alan by the hand. "Somethin's up. We better go find Mattie."

Alan stood and followed Roxie down the stairs, through the parlor where only a few of the girls milled about waiting for customers. "Go get your street clothes on and tell the other girls to do the same," Roxie hissed and waived them all out of the parlor. "I think there's gonna be trouble." The room emptied quickly, as though the women already knew about it or sensed trouble.

"What in hell's name is goin' on around here?" Roxie shouted as she pulled Alan into the unusually quiet kitchen. Roxie stopped dead in her tracks when she saw Jim Hardy with a squirming Mattie in his arms and three leering men with Minnie and her girls backed up and wide-eyed against the sinks.

"Grab the little blonde bitch," Hardy ordered. "Ramsay, you better get on outa here."

"Jim," Alan said trying to reason, "this is no way to handle things."

"Alan, I know you're sharin' this slut's bed, so don't talk to me about how to handle my business. How much of her take are you gettin' from this place or are you just happy with her asshole?"

The men holding guns on Minnie, her daughter, and her granddaughter laughed. When he turned to stare, Roxie recognized Pete. Drool ran down his stubbled chin as he laughed from his mouth that drooped noticeably on one side. Minnie and her girls stared back at Roxie with terrified expressions on their faces.

"Don't be ridiculous, Jim," Alan said and pulled Roxie a little closer to him. "You'd best take your men and get on outa here. Dewey's blabbin' all over town that something's going down here tonight. Virgil Earp and his other deputies will no doubt be here to see what's going on soon."

Hardy yanked hard on Mattie's long red hair in an effort to get her under control. "I'm gonna enjoy fuckin' all your holes, bitch," he snarled after Mattie stomped on one of his feet again. "Thelma and her girls are gonna keep Earp and his troublemakers plenty busy tonight," Hardy said with a chuckle. "She's under the impression she's gonna be able to move into this place and take over." He reached behind him and grabbed an oil lamp from the wall and tossed it over Roxie's head to smash. Oil ran down the wall to puddle on the floor. "But Thelma's mistaken," he cackled, "There's not gonna be nothin' left here but an ash filled cellar when me and the boys are done."

"Oh, dear lord," Roxie breathed and wished she had her pistols on her.

Mattie struggled harder in Hardy's grasp and he finally punched her. Roxie groaned as her friend slid to the floor unconscious.

"I'm gonna kill you, Hardy," Roxie screamed and pulled away from Alan to lunge at the big Whisky Row saloon owner.

"I seriously doubt that, bitch," Hardy snarled. "Grab her and the first man that pins her gets to fuck her first.

The men holding guns on Minnie and her girls turned and grabbed for Roxie. One of them pistol-whipped Alan and Roxie felt him go down behind her.

"Get your hands off me you addle-brained cocksucker," Roxie yelled as Pete grabbed her and swung the butt of his gun toward her jaw to pistol-whip her.

"Who's addle-brained now," Roxie heard him say before everything went black.

She didn't feel him yank open her corset and suck on her nipples or tear off her bloomers and attack what lie beneath them. She didn't hear the other men cheering him on or Minnie and her girls sobbing as both she and Mattie were violated by Hardy and his men.

Roxie came to briefly and reached for Alan's hand, but Pete kicked her in the head and sent her back into oblivion before she could grab onto it tightly. She came to again as somebody pulled her to her feet. Heat engulfed her and she could hardly breath. The acrid stench of kerosene filled her nostrils and somebody slapped a wet cloth over her face as they carried her out into the cool night air.

"Mattie," she coughed as someone wrapped her naked body in a blanket. "Where's Mattie?"

"I'm here, Rox," Mattie whispered and Roxie clutched at her friend's hand. Her red hair gleamed brightly in the glow of the flames.

Another redhead knelt at Roxie's side and held her hand. "Oh Miss Roxie," Moira sobbed, "I'm so sorry for your beautiful house."

Roxie looked up at the blaze then and understanding dawned for the first time. "Alan," she gasped and searched around her for the handsome mine owner. "Where's Alan?"

"He's alright, Rox," Mattie assured her. "They took him along with Miss Minnie and her girls over to Doc Robinson's. They breathed in some smoke, but none of them got burned."

"And Hardy?" Roxie coughed as she stared at the flames devouring her dream.

"Gone," she said and nodded her chin toward The Victoriana. "Him and his bastards. They're all burned to ashes along with our beautiful Victoriana."

"Good," she said and slipped back into unconsciousness.

Chapter 24

July 5, 1880

Roxie and Alan stood with Mattie at the train station in Phoenix. They'd ridden down with her in a stage to see her off to her new home in St. Louis. She would take a train from Phoenix to Dallas, Texas and from there she'd change trains a few times until she would finally arrive in St. Louis. It would take over a week, but wouldn't be nearly as uncomfortable or time consuming as the trip Roxie had taken to get to Prescott from Dodge four years earlier.

"Are you sure you don't want to come to St. Louis with me, Rox?" Mattie asked her closest friend of over ten years.

Roxie glanced up at the handsome face of Alan Ramsay and smiled. She twisted the diamond studded gold band on her left hand. "I think I'm gonna be just fine, now Red and so are you. Your sister and her babies are gonna get out of Kentucky and move into that big house in St. Louis, aren't they?"

"Yah," she said sadly. "It'll be good for Miriam to get away from that farm and all the sad memories there." She took a deep breath. "I just can't believe Walt is really gone."

"Who's Walt?" Alan asked as he held Roxie close.

"My sister's husband," Mattie said before Roxie could say anything. "We grew up on adjacent farms and were close as children."

"I'm so sorry," Alan said sincerely. "What happened to him?"

"He fell out of the barn and broke his leg a while back," Mattie sighed. "It never healed right and eventually he got the gangrene. He refused to let them take the leg and it killed him."

"Some men are proud that way," Alan said with a shrug.

Mattie smiled sadly. "Walt would have said a one-legged farmer wouldn't be nothing but a burden on his family."

"Sounds like he was a practical man," Alan said and took a quick sip from Roxie's flask.

"Practical and dead," Roxie said with a grunt. She looked up at Alan and frowned. "I'd much rather have a live husband than a dead one. I've already been down that road and I don't want to travel it again."

Alan furrowed his brow in confusion.

"I'll explain it all to ya on the way back up to Prescott," she said and brought his big hand up to her lips.

Acknowledgements

I'd like to take this opportunity to thank my friends at The Central Phoenix Writers' Workshop. I did this one without y'all, but if it hadn't been for all your guidance and encouragement through the first two, I would never have made it this far. Thank you from the bottom of my heart.

Without the good folks at Wikipedia this would have taken years longer. Thank you for your great service to writers like me who really hope to get the facts straight in their Historical Fiction.

That being said, I'd like to make it clear that this is a work of fiction. Prescott, Arizona, is a real place and was the first capitol of the Territory and the State of Arizona. Whiskey Row is still a spirited center of town, but the cribs and rowdy saloons have been replaced by cafes and antique shops. Virgil Earp, the famous Wyatt's brother did, indeed, live and work in Prescott. He worked at the sawmill there and was a city constable. It was his idea to have his brothers and their families search out opportunities in the new, mineral-rich territory. Doc Holliday and Katie visited Prescott and his big game at The Palace Hotel was said to have netted him close to forty thousand dollars. He and Kate slipped away into the night after the game to join Wyatt and Morgan in Tombstone, casting some suspicion on the gambler. We all know what happened in Tombstone. Doc and Kate stayed together, though in a near constant state of drunken bickering until Doc went off to Colorado without her and succumbed to his consumption. Miraculously, she never caught it from him, though they were together for close to ten years. She went on to practice the Trade across southern Arizona for several more years. Mattie Blaylock, Wyatt's common-law wife, died in the Globe,

Arizona, area of a laudanum overdose and was buried in an unmarked grave in a cemetery outside Superior, Arizona. (a mining town near Globe) Her grave was found and a marker placed there in the early 2000s by a local historical group and it is now well-tended. As Roxie predicted, Prescott was a good place for Katie to retire to. When the Arizona Pioneers' home was opened in Prescott, Kate pressured the sitting governor, a former regular client, to find her a spot there. After several years of nasty letters, he finally relented and Kate was given a room. She died there and is buried in the Pioneer's Cemetery in Prescott.

I sincerely hope you have enjoyed Mattie and Roxie's adventures across the West. It began with their meeting in *The Ruby Queen,* and continued with their life in Dodge City and their adventures in Colorado in *The Queen of the Cow Towns.* Charles Devaroe's meeting and romance with his wife Olivia plays out in *Sweet Rewards.*

Thank you all for your patronage. Please do this author one final favor and go to the review section under the books at Amazon and leave a review. If you liked the stories, tell me why. If you hated them, tell me why. As writers we cannot improve our craft if we don't know where we are falling short. Reviews are important. Amazon has a mysterious algorithm system based on the number of reviews a book receives. Please leave reviews for all the books you read, not just mine.

Made in the USA
Middletown, DE
29 July 2021